"Treasure in the Park"

A Fictional Odyssey in Christian Morals

By AL ALLAWAY

First printing, September, 2007
Second printing, January, 2008
Rewrite & third printing, November, 2019

ISBN 978-0-6151-6363-5
Published by AllawayBooks
Printed by Lulu in the United States of America www.lulu.com

FOREWORD

This author worked for many years as a volunteer in Yakima Sportsman State Park in Central Washington State, which provided the natural background for this tale. I have always been a lover of nature, an avid photographer and birdwatcher. When the opportunity arose to buy into Yakima's premier mobile home park, called Sun Country Estates, I realized the extra perks available because there was a 266 acre State Park immediately across the street.

The park boasted many species of birds, mammals and amphibians; a naturalist's paradise! Much of the state park acreage was undeveloped floodplain along the Yakima River, a place for adventure, exploration and new opportunities to bring out the lost boy that still hides in every adult male.

Thus the adventure became a 'Huckleberry Finn' fantasy. Throughout the tale to follow, the main character, Marty is doing battle with his Christian conscience regarding the rightful ownership of the substantial amount of cash that he has found.

The moral issue becomes more complicated when the cash is lost. He knows the missing money must somehow relate to other mysterious happenings in the park, but is reluctant to tell anyone because he might lose a fortune. In the end, he knows that he must trust the Lord and do the right thing. But does he?

Al Allaway Yakima, WA.

September 11, 2007

Chapter One

On the other side of the fence, a grey horse lifted its head and watched with temporary curiosity as a young boy walked through the woods toward the river.

Moonlight filtered through the trees, casting eerie patterns on the damp ground. If the horse had any knowledge of humans, it would have seemed odd that a creature so young would be alone in the woods at night. But the horse had no such intuition; sensing no danger, she put her head back down to continued grazing in the brown grasses. The gentle crop-crop of her bite could be heard for a short distance, competing with the other whispers of a nighttime forest.

A curious great-horned owl also saw the boy, but quickly determined that he was too large for prey, so swiveled its head back in the direction where a mouse had been pattering in the dry leaves. Autumn was well advanced and the faint click-click of drifting leaves striking the ground also created a rustle. The owl however was well qualified to determine the difference between the whisper of the breeze, the swish of the mouse, the soft munching of the horse and the faint click of dead dry leaves sighing as they hit the ground.

The boy moved on through the shadows and the rising evening vapors to a destination that only he knew. The mist brought with it the odor of fall; one of algae, fungi and ripe vegetation. The faint trail he followed was indistinguishable to any eye except that of a qualified woodsman. He should have tripped several times over protruding tree roots, but a seemingly supernatural force guided him safely through the gloom, always bypassing invisible thorns of berry and wild rose. He moved through the forest as if walking on air.

The lad had a purpose and a driving energy that could not be delayed by ordinary hazards. Like the owl, he too was in tune to all the night sounds around him.

He was a fair youth; some might even call him beautiful, his shining blonde hair was almost white in the moon-glow, he was aged about nine with bright blue eyes, well built and displaying a happy smile. Like the owl and the horse, we might also consider this to be an unusual place and time for a lad of this stature. He carried no pack and wore light summer clothes, barely warm enough to ward off the chill of the new night.

On this evening, the only things he carried were a can of *Dinty Moore* beef stew and an aerosol can of *Off* insect repellant.

These items had been given to him a couple of hours earlier, just before sundown, by a volunteer park ranger who had taken pity on the kid, and wondered, like the horse and the owl, just what he was doing apparently alone out in the unimproved miles of the park.

A cold shiver crept up the boy's spine as he considered another lonely night. Perhaps the shiver might have also been caused by the cool temperature, or by thoughts of biting insects.

The boy realized the value of the insect repellant because of the swarms of mosquitoes and biting flies that inhabited the area. The stew, on the other hand, created a problem for him, as he had no can-opener. He had faith that he would somehow figure out how to eat this dinner when he got to his camp. Perhaps he could puncture the can enough using a pen knife and then warm the stew over a small fire.

Gratitude flooded his heart for the kind old ranger who had provided this welcome provision. But in the morning, he would have to move his camp to a different location because surely that ranger would be asking questions, checking with authorities and probably searching for the lad. Besides which, he knew that this was State Park land and camping was prohibited except in designated areas.

# # #

Marty Bart unlocked the shop door and stepped inside. The place was musty and smelled of sour mops, moldy hay, engine oil and chemicals. This building was of logs, constructed more than 100 years earlier and held many odors of the past. It had once been a hunting lodge. Windows were now so covered with cobwebs that little light penetrated through the decades of accumulated dust. It was indeed a dreary and musty place. He hung up his coveralls, leaf rake and back-pack chemical sprayer.

Marty's eyes burned and he felt a choking dryness in his throat, but these symptoms did not concern him... not much, anyway. Whenever he stirred up fine dust by raking dried leaves and debris from around the bases of the park's giant trees, he would experience the same discomfort. Some of the trees were so ancient that humps of roots kept mowers at a distance. He had been working at this chore for almost a week. The raking had to be done so that a chemical could be applied to the bare earth to sterilize and prevent future weed seed growth in areas where the mowers could not reach..

His boss, the Head Ranger, was always expounding on the dangers of *hanta virus* and other respiratory threats, but Marty considered the offered face mask to be a nuisance, and seldom complied with the safety rule, especially if the boss wasn't around.

At seventy-five, Marty figured that he'd been blessed with good health all of his life and he could afford to take chances with such minor things as mouse feces.

True, there were lots of rodents especially little deer mice in the park and they were a known carrier and spreader of the virus, but Marty had more weighty thoughts chewing in his brain besides *hanta virus*. Life's little threats were so numerous and common that if a man dwelt on each one he'd have no time for the good things of life.

Hanging up the last of his gear, prior to quitting for the day, Marty recalled some of the more serious events of this day; things that had been most extraordinary. Nothing exciting ever happened in this park, usually... But today would be a day the old timer's would be talking about for years to come.

There was a retirement home down the road from the park, and he could imagine the patriarchs sitting in their rocking chairs speculating about the dead body. The Sheriff's deputies said that it had probably been a murder. The body was that of a muscular young man, in his mid twenties, found dead in the park's day use showers first thing that morning. Marty hadn't seen it but heard all about it from the old geezer who discovered the corpse.

Old Tom Morris from the retirement home, walked in the park every morning before breakfast, rain or shine. He and Marty were old friends, bonded in a special brotherhood, Tom was Marty's Lieutenant when Marty was a rookie Firefighter. Both retired from the city fire department years earlier.

Ending his hike, Tom stopped to use the restroom, and there it was! A pale and naked cadaver sitting in the corner on the shower floor, propped up against the wall, grinning at him like a Cheshire cat. Poor Tom probably thought he was going to have a heart attack. When the Detectives and the Coroner finished all their questions, Tom was still stiffly glued to the bench outside the men's room and Marty had to call the nurse from the old-age home to come get him. He'd missed his breakfast and would have missed lunch also.

The Head Ranger and a couple of aides then scrubbed out the shower stall and tidied things up. One of the four showers had to be closed because vandals had ripped out the water meter coin box.

Marty, being an unpaid volunteer was not needed and did not offer to help. He specialized in specific projects of his own choosing, like trail building and maintenance, map making and grounds upkeep. Sometimes, he dreamt that he might be paid for his many hours of work as he and his disabled wife barely made ends meet on his feeble fire service pension. But job satisfaction and "good-job" praise were sufficient rewards.

After lunch, when things were quiet again, Marty was back to work, raking leaves. This was his favorite part of the job, not so much the work and the dust, but the seclusion. Being far out away from driveways, trails and people gave him great opportunity to commune with God and to enjoy the great natural gifts that He has given to us out of His love, for us to enjoy.

Like the child of his youth, Marty enjoyed shuffling through deep piles of yellow and red leaves. On this day he paused to look skyward to see perfect wedges of Canada geese honking their way in southern flight. It might turn out to be a joyful day after all.

He had to resist the kid in him urging him to lie down and roll in the deep piles. That would have been a little too far beneath his dignity.

After the hunting preserve sold out, parts of this State Park had once been an arboretum, so now the leaf shapes and colors offered a much greater variety. Many species of trees had been planted from all over the world, outnumbering the few native species. As a result, one green-black leaf among all the reds and oranges did not particularly stand out, and Marty almost missed it.

He was raking a three foot wide perimeter around an ancient oak tree, whose leaves had not yet fallen. Yellow maple leaves had blown there in last night's wind. The green-grey leaf was definitely out of place, but the sight of it did not reach Marty's brain until after he had buried it in a pile of cleared leaves. Curiosity delayed, he propped his rake against the trunk and knelt down to further investigate.

"Probably just a gum wrapper or some other trash." He told himself. Sifting further, his heart took a leap as he looked at a piece of greenback currency. He had to blink twice to verify what he thought he had seen. There were, in fact, TWO Zeros after the ONE. *"How in the world did a one-hundred dollar bill get lost in the park?"*

Marty tweaked the bill between his thumb and forefinger, feeling the weave of the fabric. A twinge of guilt began to emerge in his mind. Somebody had obviously lost this money and may have greater need of it than he. Marty had a compassionate heart, always sensitive to the needs of others and his conscience was immediately searching for ways to return it. Glancing about, he saw no one any where near. Fragments of a Bible Scripture crept into his head; something about riches profit nothing but righteousness saves from death.

There was a time frame when Marty had no doubt what he would do with the bill, obviously return it to its' owner, but as time moved forward, the doubt grew and became eroded.

Before putting the bill in his wallet, he observed that it was quite tattered and torn. Rationalizing his choices, he considered that probably been chewed up by a lawnmower, therefore had been lying around for a month or more. Logic argued that the owner didn't care, or they would have been looking during the past weeks. The mowers had not been cutting grass for at least three weeks. The more he thought about the options, the further away the moral issue became. The thought of trying to return the bill to its rightful owner faded to nothing. Besides, he really needed the money to meet his bills this month. After all, he reasoned, if God let him find this treasure, how could God be offended if he kept it?

Feeling happy and a little smug, Marty finished up the section he had set up for his goal for the day. He was at the very end of the groomed lawns, right at the edge of unimproved areas, often referred to as "wilderness". This State Park covered many square miles, much of it used only by native wildlife. He stood there momentarily watching a family of deer, grazing peacefully nearby.

Suddenly, the deer spooked and bolted off into the thick brush. Marty knew that it was not his presence that caused them alarm because he was a frequent visitor and these deer were almost like pets. Something had startled them and Marty wondered what or who. So, he hung back to watch for a few minutes. Sure enough, he caught a glimpse of something red coming toward him through the trees and brush.

Separated by only a rail fence, a young boy in a red shirt walked up to Marty. He was the fairest kid Marty had ever seen.

He had bright blond hair reminding Marty of an eight-year old cherub with a gentle face, almost generating an ethereal glow. Marty could almost visualize wings on an angel.

"Hello," said the boy, in a voice almost like tinkling bells. His smile was sincere and infectious, but with an authority of a much older person.

"Hello, yourself," answered Marty. "Are you hiking?"

"No, but can I fish in your pond?"

"I dunno," teased Marty, "Are you under fourteen?"

"Thirteen," said the lad.

Marty raised his brows, thinking this kid could not be more than ten, more likely about eight. "You don't have a fishing pole," he observed.

"It's over behind the pond."

"Oh!" Just then, a distant shout briefly distracted Marty, who turned away to see who was calling. It was the Chief Ranger who motioned for Marty to come to him. Marty waved back in compliance then turned to speak again to the boy...

Gone! Completely vanished! Marty drifted his eyes in all directions finding no sign of the kid. Marty had been distracted for less than three seconds, a time too impossibly short for the kid to disappear. A mystery! Did he imagine the kid? Was the kid some kind of a spirit or something?

# # #

That night, the corpse, the cash and the child kept popping up and disturbing Marty's attempt to find sleep. All three of the day's monumental events started with a "C". Intuitively, he assumed that they must somehow be related, but that idea defied all logic. He kept drifting back to the cash. One-hundred dollar bills were extremely rare, seldom used by the common population. In fact, he had only seen one other in his entire life. Drug dealers or bank robbers were the only people who handled that kind of money. That would be true if one believed everything the media expounded.

Most people who came to the State Park were there because they could not afford to pay for entertainment. Access was free and attracted bus loads of school children and low income families seeking inexpensive picnic parties for birthdays or anniversaries. In the depth of winter, it was the only free and safe place for ice skaters. The only fishing allowed was for kids, 14 and under. Sometimes bird-watchers trekked through, but Marty had never heard of a wealthy bird-watcher.

As he finally drifted off to a troubled sleep, it occurred to him that the bill might be counterfeit; maybe play money lost from some kid's game. In the morning, he would take it to the bank to see if it was actually real... or... n...o..t...

#

It took most of the morning to visit two medical providers where Marty's wife Beth was receiving treatments for nerve and tendon disorders. Good doctors were becoming scarce, as many now refused to take on new patients if under Medicare. As Beth's condition deteriorated, it became more and more difficult to afford adequate care.

There was also some shopping they had to do. Then, while Beth waited in the car, there was the bank teller who looked at Marty with askance suspicion when he deposited one very ratty looking one-hundred dollar bill.

"Looks real to me," she said. "Did you find it somewhere?"

"Uhuh." he wasn't sure why, but he wanted to get out of the bank as quickly as possible.

It was late afternoon before Marty was finally able to seek out the seclusion of work in the State Park. Back where the kid had spooked the deer on the previous day, he propped his rake against a tree and climbed through the rail fence to have a look around. For several hours memories of the young boy had been consuming his curiosity. He had already walked around the fishing pond and could find no evidence of recent activity.

Fifty feet or so from the fence, Marty found a small clearing, and on the ground a most curious array.

Dirt had been smoothed like play sand in a sandbox. Lemons and pine cones and apple cores were half buried in the dirt. They were arranged like toy soldiers on a make believe battlefield, six lemons on one side, six apple cores on the other with two pine cones backing up each side, possibly representing artillery or a commanding general.

Marty, intently studying the layout, was suddenly startled by a voice inches behind him.

"Hello," said the lad. His voice was the same, soft like tinkling bells.

Marty jumped, "You startled me," he said. "Were you hiding behind a tree?"

"No."

"Do you live around here?"

"No. I'm camped down by the river."

"In the State Park?" asked Marty

"Dunno," said the boy. He was still wearing the same red shirt which made a startling contrast with his angel-bright blue eyes and the late afternoon sun reflected like a golden halo off his blonde hair.

Again Marty recalled his thoughts of the previous day suggesting an ethereal spirit.

"Are you alone?" queried Marty.

"Nope, but my folks are working right now," said the boy. "Do you have anything to eat?"

Marty replied, "I keep some cookies and some canned beef stew in my car in case I meet up with any homeless people. Are you homeless?"

"Nah, but I'm awfully hungry."

Feeling that food would help to keep this mysterious youngster talking, Marty said. "If you want, I'll walk out and get some. You wait right here." Marty turned to leave.

"Mister...?"

"My name is Marty."

"The mosquitoes are awfully bad. Do you have any spray?"

"Sure. I'll be back in ten minutes."

Marty left his rake and back-pack sprayer and walked back to his parked car. Rummaging through the trunk, he located two cans of *Dinty-Moore* stew. Taking his time, he wanted to think about what to say or how to get more information from the lad. He could warn him that camping is prohibited both in the park and on adjoining land.

And then, there was cranky old Punch Jacobs who bred horses on property adjoining the park. He'd been known to fire a load of buckshot before asking questions, so if they were indeed camping, it would have to be one place or the other.

Shadows were beginning to lengthen when Marty returned with the stew, and the kid was nowhere to be seen. Vanished again, like a wraith, he was! He called out, producing no answer. It was then that Marty noticed his rake was gone. Twirling around, he discovered the back-pack sprayer was also missing.

Not sure what to do, Marty went through the rail fence to where the toy battleground had been set up. There was his rake, and all traces of the lemons and pine cones were gone. The ground had been raked clean.

Still not fully convinced the kid was a thief, Marty's big heart decided to leave the stew and bug spray in case the boy returned. If he didn't, it could always be recovered on another day.

Walking back to the car, Marty considered the best way to tell the Head Ranger that the sprayer, park property, had been stolen. He concluded that the only tale he could tell would have to be the truth. But, even that became moot, for when he reached the car, there sat his tank and sprayer, leaning neatly against the car, just as pretty as you please!

Chapter Two

At about four hours past midnight, a shadowy figure exited from a black sedan that had been parked a couple of blocks south of the parks gated entrance. Only a face was visible under a black stocking cap. The person carefully latched the car door so as to make as little noise as possible. Strolling north to the gate, the figure was barely visible, dark clothes blending easily with background shadows on this moonless night.

Easily climbing the gate, the individual by-passed the caretaker's residence then made a beeline straight to the juvenile fishing pond. Once there, a flashlight was produced and the dark form began searching the shallow water amongst the reeds and rushes along the ponds edge. The hunt took about an hour and resulted in the removal of a white plastic box, wrapped in waterproof oilcloth. Once the item was recovered, the figure unwrapped it, then dumped it back into the pond and retreated rapidly back to the black sedan.

The driver of the black sedan was not aware that two bald men had been watching from an old VW van and followed, minus headlights, as the sedan drove off. It was an hour before sunrise. The back of the van was painted with anti-Semitic symbols and a Nazi swastika.

# # #

Metro Detective Sergeant Anne Lee studied photographs of the latest murder corpse and furrowed her brow. "Is there any word yet from the M.E.?"

"No," replied her partner, "but the Feds just called and think they can I. D. our John Doe."

"How'd they get involved?"

"Dunno, but they've got an agent down at the morgue right now, and guess what else?"

"Hit me with it!"

"It's not the F.B.I., but people from Homeland Security. There was some mention of terrorism."

"Geez," ventured Anne, "how does terrorism figure in the State Park? Has anybody informed the Ranger?"

"They said to wait until they get here," replied her partner.

Chapter Three 🏕

The next time Marty reported for raking duty, it became instantly apparent something was missing. His firefighter brother, Tom Morris was nowhere to be seen. Tom walked in the park seven mornings out of seven and always looked forward to meeting with Marty to shoot a little bull. Some of the memories they would share were becoming tarnished by repetition, but what were memories for, anyway?

Marty missed Tom and resolved to check up on him at the retirement home later in the day. It would be easy to suspect yesterday's murder was too much for the frail old man. Maybe Marty could make time later to go play a few games of checkers.

On this day reporting to work his attention was directed in different directions. Whenever one piece of money is found outdoors, hope is always generated and the eye wants to automatically seek out the possibility of more, and he was anxious to rake around more trees.

However, the Head Ranger wanted more information about the boy and the body and intercepted Marty before he could begin work.

Sitting in the office, waiting was wearing on Marty's patience. Marty didn't have much to offer and grew impatient, especially when the boss got busy on the phone or chatting with visitors. The man was super gregarious and loved to talk. Marty would glance at him questioningly, hoping to get away to his own little world.

"Sit down and wait a minute, Marty," he would say. "I won't be long." But, he'd talk on and on.

Wasted time bothered Marty's conscience. Nathan the Head Ranger finally finished his casual chitchat with the person on the phone, and gave his long overdue attention to Marty.

"So, tell me more about these people camping illegally in the park," he started.

"I haven't seen any evidence at all," said Marty. "Every time the kid tells me something, I check it out. When he said he was fishing, I checked all around the pond and there were no footprints anywhere. It rained last week and nobody has been over there since, except me. The kid said his name was Nick and that his folks were working during the day, but if they are camping out there somewhere, they'd have to come through the park, or fly like birds." Thinking quick like a stand-up comic, he added, "Maybe old man Jacobs got 'em with a load of buckshot! Ha!"

"Maybe they're all angels," kidded Nathan.

"Funny you should say that," said Marty. "The way that kid keeps popping up unexpectedly, then seemingly vanishing into thin air led me to believe he could be something supernatural. And then there are his looks; like a little cherub, he is and always smiling. Nothing about him suggests he's an ordinary kid."

Marty didn't mention the cones, cores and lemons on the pretend battlefield.

"Have we checked everywhere on the island?" asked Ranger Nathan.

"All except the south end."

"Well, let's suspend your leaf raking for today. Why don't you take a long hike and check out the whole area? Take along a radio and keep me advised."

"Okay," said Marty. "Have you heard anything more from the police about the body?"

"Nope."

"You don't suppose there's any chance the two incidents could be related, do you?"

"That's an interesting theory," replied Nathan.

# # #

Marty had much to ponder on his way to the area they called "the island". It wasn't really an island at all, except when the river flooded. When that happened each spring season, the so-called "wilderness" parts of the park became numerous sloughs and backwater creating many islands, all still under the canopy of huge old trees.

Marty was disappointed to be side-tracked on this new mission. It was not what he had planned. Chief in his mind was the problem the money now seemed to create. It could easily be an important clue relating to the murder, and Marty knew it. He was dwelling on this fact as his conscience gnawed deeper into his soul. He already had spent the money on Beth's medical bills and to mention it now would just add further complications. He kept telling himself that the bill had been in the park long before the body was found, and almost a mile away. The rationalized result was that there was no way they could relate, therefore Marty would not mention it to anyone.

That settled, he started to whistle as he picked his way along the trail and onto the "island". Marty often whistled while walking or working deep in the woods. Sometimes he imitated bird calls and was pretty good at it, proven by the fact that many of the birds answered his call. He bragged to anyone who would listen about the osprey he had once coaxed out of the sky to land on the beach only a few feet from where he was seated on a log. Marty said that version of the call was of a baby bird in distress and that was how he was able to fool the adult osprey.

Marty knew much of the island like the back of his hand. He had first explored the area as a teenager, some sixty years earlier. Seasonal floods had changed it many times before it was annexed to the State Park system. After the devastating flood of '96 he had been the driving force behind enlisting volunteers to help restore it.

It was Marty's survey the park had adopted to build a new trail system and most of the ten miles of trail had been personally cleared by him. Budget constraints in the State Legislature had dictated that the restoration of this flood-plain would have to be done solely by volunteer labor, if done at all.

Today, his first stop was to check a fox den. Earlier in the spring he had played nurse maid to a widowed red fox by supplementing her food supply while she weaned her kits. The relationship had blossomed almost to the point where the fox trusted Marty enough to come within ten feet of him if he was sitting still. She was beautiful and most curious.

Illegal game poaching was always a problem on State Park lands, but why anyone would shoot Mr. Fox and just let the carcass and the fur rot, was beyond him. Wild game was scarce enough here without the addition of wanton waste.

Moving on toward the south, Marty was aware of every sound. Nothing escaped his keen sharp senses. There was not a rabbit, deer or woodpecker that could venture a quick peek around a tree, without him being aware of its presence. No natural smell, sound or plant was unknown to him. The previous year, he had worked with members of the Native Plant Society to categorize the entire native flora that grew in the area. He and wife Beth were avid birders, and participated annually in the Audubon Society's Christmas bird counts.

This "island wilderness" was endearing to him in other ways. There was a wonderful special place, known only to him and Beth. Due to poor health, she could no longer walk the distance, which saddened them both.

The treasure here was the memory of their first kiss, followed two years later by a proposal of marriage. Marty came here often; anytime he needed quality time with God; anytime conflict developed in his large family. It was the one place where he could dream about happier times and seek answers from solitude.

Suddenly, he caught a flash of red moving through the trees, and was jerked unceremoniously back to the present. It was the boy, still wearing a red shirt.

"Hey! Stop," he hollered. "Let's talk!"

Either the boy was too far away to hear, or chose to ignore the command, so Marty started after, running as fast as his 75 years would allow. The boy quickly outdistanced him and Marty had to stop to catch his breath. After a short pause, he started on again, slower this time, planning to use his tracking skills instead of trying to outrun the kid.

He could locate an occasional smudge of a footprint here and there, but after a hundred yards, Marty could find no trace of the lad. The direction he had been going didn't make any sense, either, as it led straight into the rushing rapids of the river. Like a wraith, the kid had vanished, again!

Marty spent the rest of the morning searching the entire area for a campsite. He located a couple of very old campfire pits, built by poachers or fishermen, but none that could have been used within the past month. He radioed Nathan that he had found nothing and that he was returning to the main park.

Again, Marty's intended goal was further delayed when Nathan asked if he could swing by the lower channel of the fishing pond. Beavers had blocked the drainage again, and it needed to be opened, otherwise the pond level would rise and the water would flood some picnic areas.

"Got it, Mean Boss," replied Marty. "Is the pitchfork still stashed out there?"

"Should be right where we hid it."

On the way to the pond, Marty slipped back into his day dream. He had been an awkward young man, just out of the Navy, when he first saw Beth ice skating on that very pond. He had watched her warming by a fire; the most magnificent young woman he had ever seen. His whole life would revolve around finding ways to get up enough courage to ask her for a date. More than fifty wonderful years had passed since.

When Marty reached the pond, it was immediately apparent that something was very wrong. Fish were floating belly up, as were a few geese. Walking on, he found a fairly substantial beaver dam, reinforced with the bodies of six dead beaver. Using the pitchfork left there for that purpose, he opened the channel, allowing the water level to drop. Whatever was killing the wildlife would be determined by the Fish and Game lab.

Finally, after lunch, Marty was back raking leaves around the base of large trees, so that the ground could be sterilized against weed growth. His minds-eye and his imagination was busy picking up more "green" out of the yellow and brown leaves.

He was in a kind of a trance and almost missed it. Was his imagination working overtime, or was that really another bill? His day-dream was shattered by the shrill chatter of a chickaree, one of the park's many squirrels.

Marty startled, looked up at the scolding mammal that was only a couple of feet above and was obviously upset about something. It was digging on a limb just a few inches from a large tree cavity that it had taken over as its home. Something was definitely on the limb that the squirrel was trying to dislodge. As it fluttered to the ground, Marty saw green. The object landed in the leaves alongside another just like the one Marty had imagined seeing only seconds before.

He blinked in conscious unbelief. There on the ground before him were two additional one-hundred dollar bills!

"Viola!" he cried aloud, and the squirrel startled and scurried back into the safety of its cavity. Leaves in the area were piled six to eight inches deep, and before long, Marty had shed the back-pack and was busy raking and sifting leaves many feet from the areas that needed to be sprayed. After an hour, on hands and knees, he had found nothing more. It was time to apply logic and look up.

It was obvious to Marty that his next move was to have a look inside the squirrel's cavity, but it was too high to search without the use of a ladder.

By now that brain mechanism called "hope for more" was running rampant and he was becoming more and more excited. His excitement however also bred caution as he realized that the use of a ladder in broad daylight would generate questions; questions for which he would have no truthful answer.

His thoughts were racing: *If there were three, there just 'gotta be more!*

Marty looked from the now scolding squirrel to a whole basketball team warming up in one direction and to a mom and her three children playing badminton on another court. The playgrounds were crowded with people so he decided to pick up his tools and quit for the day. It was the only ruse available to him.

# # #

Nathan Peterschwarz spent his entire working life in the State Park System. He was a large and muscular man who loved the outdoors. Sometimes he regretted taking the managerial position because it kept him indoors pushing paper more than he liked. From the Ranger station he would watch his staff with envy while they went about doing various chores. He had degrees in Forestry and Wildlife Biology and would love to leave his computer, put on coveralls to test a tree for insect infestation or crawl under one of the tractors or mowers to squirt a little grease.

He was now in that critical mid-point of his life, where a man wonders if he chose the right profession, the right spouse, the right investments or the right pension. Debt was another factor. Doubts about the future tend to create wanderlust, more so at his age.

Nathan was deeply in love with his wife, but that did not stop his eyes from wandering over the figures of younger women. Another popular word for this condition is, "mid-life crisis." Nathan would never violate his wedding vows, but his alter-ego was in constant conflict.

Nate, as he wanted to be called by his park staff, commanded the careers of thirteen full time rangers, whose ranks swelled to almost thirty when temporary aides joined the staff in the summertime. In addition, four area residents enjoyed the park enough to serve as year-round volunteers. Marty was the most dependable of these, and he had been nominated for volunteer of the year awards on several occasions. Beth's cousin John also donated carpentry and electrical skills.

On this day, Nate was in a deep funk. Depression was not something he usually experienced, but he had just received notice of a huge budget reduction, effective immediately.

The State Legislature was always looking for a scape-goat when it came to saving a little money, and the Parks System was always the first in their cross hairs. But, this cut didn't make any sense; it would be a disaster, cutting Nate's resources by almost fifty per cent.

If he couldn't figure out alternatives, it would mean laying off half of his people. It was going to be a king-sized dilemma; how to manage 200 campsites, over 100 acres of groomed day use areas, twenty three miles of foot and bridle trails, two miles of riverfront, and huge wildlife management areas; fencing around a total of twelve square miles, all in the middle of a sprawling major city.

Nate looked out of his office window at a cottontail rabbit gamboling with a covey of quail. It was sunny and warm for a mid November day, and Nate felt overwhelmed with his management responsibilities. He grumbled to himself, *Why me?*

Picking up a telephone, he dialed the home number from the top of a list; a long list of his assistant rangers. He had built an effective team and now, had the unpleasant task of tearing it apart. Who would he layoff first?

# # #

Well after twilight, Marty parked his car in an out of the way dead-end street. He knew several ways to access the park, without being seen. He wore black pants, a dark sweater and gloves. Without a ski-mask, he still felt like a sneaky burglar. He carried a six foot step ladder and disappeared into the night. His route led for a half mile along the flood control dike that separated the groomed parts of the park from the many miles of flood plain and wilderness areas.

Lightning was flashing from an approaching storm and the wind was becoming severe. The night was sultry and would soon generate torrents of rain.

Marty heard the crack of a falling limb somewhere off in the darkness and thought he might need to abort this search in favor of another time, but the urgency of the mission and his demand for answers spurred him on in spite of any danger. Another tree fell to the ground with a loud crash and he could feel the vibrations through the earth. If there were any stubborn leaves left, this wind would certainly dislodge them.

Then it started to rain and a third tree snapped under the wind pressure and fell to the earth.

Marty was off the dike and within a few feet of his target, so he decided to continue his quest. Lightning flashed again as Marty reached the squirrel's tree.

He set up his aluminum step ladder and sent up a brief prayer that any lightning strike would not hit this tree at this time.

At last, thought Marty, *I'll know one way or the other.* His heart was pounding as he climbed up to the first branch, reaching a position where he could shine a flashlight into the cavity.

Just then, however, his eyes detected other lights moving through the trees perhaps a hundred yards away. There were two people, each with flashlights, walking toward the fishing pond.

Marty doused his light, not wanting anyone to know where he was or what he was doing. No one was permitted in this part of the park after the gates closed at dusk.

Frozen against the trunk of the tree, he watched the mysterious figures until they passed out of his view.

Who they were and why they were here would be a question of concern later. Right now, Marty's attention was focused elsewhere. With each flash of lightning, he searched other directions for any signs of other intruders.

He shuddered with a new chill and realized that he was soaking wet. Finally, feeling secure, he recovered his purpose and his flashlight, peering into the cavity...

And there it was...

Three tightly tied bundles...

Bundles of United States of America currency. Some of it was partially buried under the squirrel's winter stash of Douglas fir seed cones, mixed with a few acorns.

The cavity's occupant, whose housekeeping efforts started this whole mystery, was nowhere to be seen.

Marty cautiously reached into the opening. Each packet of bills was about two and a half inches thick, showing one hundred dollars on the outside of each.

It seemed anticlimactic to simply place the packets in a pocket of his vest, climb down off the ladder, fold it up and retreat back towards his parked car. It had been too easy!

Rain had been falling steady for almost an hour when Marty earlier climbed the side of the dike, about twenty feet from the squirrel's tree. A blinding flash had illuminated the scene.

Marty wasn't sure which came first; the lightning or the deafening noise. For a fraction of a second he felt a tingle where he held the aluminum ladder, dropping it milliseconds before the tree crashed down on top of him, squishing his body into the mud of the dike.

A thousand bright points of multi-colored light flashed on Marty's brain and then there was nothing but stygian darkness.

# # #

Nicolas Fix was also soaking wet, hidden in a makeshift vine hut. Plastic sheets over his head were insufficient to keep out the wind driven rain. The groan of the wind rose to a shriek while falling limbs and sometimes whole trees added a staccato like cannon gunfire. Nick moved his sleeping bag for the fourth time attempting to find the driest spot in his tiny shelter. Nick prayed for protection from the falling debris. He shivered from the cold as well as from fright. All he could do was dream of a better life... someday!

Chapter Four

Nicholas Fix was hungry again. Worse than that, he was always hungry. Winter was coming and he would have to be seeking more adequate shelter. The nights were already cold, the temperature falling well below freezing. The temperature of the late fall days would no longer rise above 50 degrees so he was always cold. The lowering angle of the sun offered none of the warmth of previous weeks.

Nick had moved his camp three times now, especially after that kind, but snoopy volunteer ranger had almost caught him out on the island. The boy had become very adept at making camp in the most unlikely places; under logs or in dense tangles of brush. Life had now evolved into an almost unbearable sequence of disappointments, nothing even close to Nick's earlier and happier years. At his tender young age, he was no stranger to hardship and privation.

It was becoming more and more obvious to park staff that the boy Nick probably didn't have parents camping in the park, that he was alone there and possibly a runaway. Ranger Nathan alerted all of his staff to keep an eye out for the kid and to try to get more information from him. He would also be checking with the local police authority in case they were looking for a runaway. Nathan then issued cameras to the on-duty staff.

That same morning, Michael, one of the full-time aides spotted the boy fishing on the opposite side of the pond. He waved and the kid waved back.

Michael then ducked into the brush, attached a telephoto lens and took six photos. Then he sought out an unmarked and hidden trail to the back side of the pond, thinking to come up on the kid and surprise him. When he arrived at the spot, there was no kid, no fishing pole and no sign of any footprints. When he shared this mystery with the boss, Nathan was puzzled.

"Well, at least we got some pictures that might help make clear his identity," he said.

"Right," answered Michael, "I'll take the film straight to the police lab. You might call Marty so he can confirm this to be the same kid."

"Come to think of it, I haven't seen Marty this morning. I'll give his home a call." Nathan didn't give it a second thought when there was no answer at Marty's home.

# # #

The red fox was patrolling the dike, followed by her two kits, looking for any morsel that might be available. It was in the hour just after dawn and the rain had stopped. Winds had scattered debris, limbs and sometimes whole trees and the foxes had to dodge in and out of it. She was looking for dislodged bird eggs or any other creature that might have been injured by the storm.

Suddenly, she stopped and emitted a low growl, warning to her offspring. There was the smell of a human nearby and that raised a flag of caution. The human smell also evoked a sense of familiarity and of pleasure. It was the same man who had shown kindness by providing food when she was weaning her kits. The fox overcame instinctive fear and approached a little closer. She strained to get a better sniff of the creature that was pinned under a huge tree. It was still alive, breathing very shallow and very unconscious. The fox edged a little closer and her kits abandoning their caution, also approached. They sniffed closer and closer...

Out of the cold and darkness, Marty felt some pleasant warmth and moisture on his neck and ear, like a faint breath of summer. Wanting more, he urged himself into a state of semi-consciousness.

Warm breath from the curious fox had an ambrosia effect. But then the pain hit.

Almost losing awareness, Marty fought back and found that he could move an arm. Otherwise, he was held down by some heavy weight. A glimmer of consciousness returned and he realized where he was and what had happened. He needed help and he needed it bad.

The loose arm felt its way in an arc to see how far it could move and fingers grasped a familiar feeling object. It was Marty's cell phone. He couldn't move the arm enough to see the phone. Hoping it still had battery life, he located the button where the nine should be and pressed it.

Most cell phones are pre-programmed for a single nine stroke. If the mini computer chip still worked it should dial 9-1-1.

Not knowing if it worked or not, he spoke his location three or four times and then faded back into unconsciousness. The last thing he remembered were his friends, the red foxes walking away. Curiously, it stuck in his brain that both kits were male.

# # #

"The film you sent in this morning was blank," the Deputy Sheriff was saying, "Either the lab fogged it, or your man left the lens cap on."

"There was no lens cap," said Nathan defensively.

"We think the child's name is Nicholas Fix," continued the Deputy, "and there's a felony fugitive warrant out for him from Idaho."

Nathan didn't want to share his feelings that this angel-like kid couldn't possibly be a wanted fugitive, so he said nothing.

"You guys are sure getting the incidents, lately," the Deputy droned on... all your vandalism reports, petty thefts, dead bodies in the shower, harboring fugitives, trees falling on volunteers..."

"What did you say?" The last four words were news to the Ranger.

"Yeah, didn't they call you? Last night's wind storm knocked a tree down on your man Marty out on the dike. The paramedics picked him up this morning."

Nathan glared at the Deputy...

"He's in a light coma, over at St. Joes..."

Nathan was out the door before the Deputy could finish his sentence.

# # #

Christmas music drifted down the hall of the hospital and into Marty's room. Wife Beth sat in a bedside straight-back chair, one hand entwined in his, her head resting on the hospital bed and she was in a light sleep when Marty stirred, opened his eyes and groaned. She was instantly alert, cried out and planted a big kiss on his face.

"Where ...?"

"Darlin', I've been so worried. You had a bad knock on the head... Been here in the hospital for ten days... Not like you to miss

Thanksgiving..." She was crying, testing his reflexes, not quite sure what to say.

"My vest...? The money...?"

"You are still delirious. You rest while I call the doctor."

Coma ended, full recovery expected, life is good, many friends visiting.

A week after his release from the hospital, Marty was healing fine in the body, but his mind was a mess. What happened to all the money? How could he ask anyone about it?

Did the paramedics steal it, or maybe the admitting nurse? His volunteer park vest was also missing, and that was where he had hidden the three packets of bills. He freely asked around about the vest, but nobody had seen it. *A likely story,* he thought.

All of his other clothes, watch and possessions from the night of the accident, were in his locker at the hospital. His wallet was there including the last two 100-dollar bills that he had extracted from out of the leaves. He was beginning to think he might have dreamt about his invasion of the squirrel's cavity.

During his physical and mental recovery, he even thought that maybe God was punishing him for not reporting the money. Why else was the tree struck by lightning only seconds after he took the money? Of all the directions the tree could have fallen, why did it fall only on him? Now, with the money missing, his dilemma was all the more severe. He had to constantly remind himself that, according to the Bible, God is pure love and does not punish. It was his own conscience that was punishing him.

On his first day back in the park, Marty strolled over to the scene of his 'accident'. Park staff had removed all traces of the storm, except for the large lower trunk of the downed tree. He poked around inside the now vacant squirrel's cavity and found nothing that might help solve his mental anxiety.

He did find a small zip-lock bag containing a strange looking playing card with a picture of a man hanging in a noose. It appeared to be totally irrelevant so he jammed it into the back pocket of his work coveralls and promptly forgot all about it.

Up on the dike, he tried to piece together the scenario of his rescue. Why had nobody asked about the ladder he had been carrying? He had been so concerned with the missing money that several days passed before the question of the ladder occurred to him. Now, he found the answer. Either the falling tree or a careless paramedic had kicked the ladder over the side of the bank, where it still lay, mostly hidden in brush. It had been a miracle that the park staff hadn't seen it when they were cleaning up the storm debris. Otherwise, there would be questions for which Marty could not provide an honest answer.

Another thought occurred to him, maybe staff members did know about the ladder and were waiting to see if Marty would 'fess up. Playing games? It was a real dilemma.

Now Marty had renewed hope. Maybe his vest (and the money) had also been slung over the bank by the force of the falling tree. But the more he considered it, the more illogical it became. Still, he had a nagging feeling that he was overlooking something very obvious, but he couldn't quite grasp what it was.

He spent another hour searching the vicinity before he finally gave up.

Just before lunch, Ranger Nathan told Marty to go get a bite to eat and then return to the conference building for a special detail.

"What is it?" Marty was curious."

"Show you when you get there," said Nate,

"It'll be an easy job. Meet me there at 1:30 promptly."

Marty lived just a couple of blocks from the park entrance and when he got home, he noticed that Beth was gone. *Probably to the therapy pool,* he conjectured.

Still pouring over all the different possibilities about the missing money, he prepared to build one of his favorite open faced toasted sandwiches. He usually made his own lunch and preferred being alone in the kitchen. His two faithful little dogs were the only exception. They knew what was about to happen and were more than ready to help Marty celebrate his lunch break.

"Today, I think it will be an over-the-sink sandwich," he told the two pooches.

They wagged as if they totally understood, and maybe they did.

Any sandwich moist enough to drip, was an 'over-the-sink" creation. When 'drier' sandwich makings were used, Marty would

sit at the kitchen table to eat, but most of his creations were eaten over the sink in order to avoid cleaning up the drips.

Their dogs were both female Shi-tzus. The oldest was really a mix of something else. She was named Me-tzu and had been purchased from a Shi-tzu breeder, who turned out to be of questionable repute. As Me-tzu grew from puppy hood it had become more and more apparent that she was not purebred.

When at the vet for her 4-month booster shots, the vet asked, "What breed is this?" Then he said, "She has a face like a Papillon."

Marty, always quick, replied, "That's right, she's a Pappy-Shi Tz." Without batting an eye, that's what the vet wrote down in the chart. Marty thought he was being funny, but the vet still had him guessing.

The younger dog was pure-bred and named Precious, which indeed, she was.

Marty finished his drippy sandwich, sharing some of it with his friends and then returned to the park. When driving through the front gate, he thought it odd the office, Ranger station and shop buildings were all dark and appeared to be locked. Of twelve other workers, not one was visible anywhere.

Obediently, at 1:30, Marty entered the park's conference building.

"Surprise!" Fifty voices cheered in unison, "Hooray for this year's Volunteer of the Year." Marty blinked, and looked around the circle of friendly faces. Unusual for him, he was at a loss for words. This was a large state with hundreds of parks, using thousands of volunteers, and they were saying that he was Number One!

Usually he was quick with a clever or ingenious reply, but today his mouth fell open and he stared around the room in genuine surprise. Wit totally escaped him.

"The word came down today from the State Capitol," Nathan said, "And I can't think of anyone who deserves it more."

"Congratulations, Darlin'," Marty's wife Beth stood beside Nathan. Behind her stood three of their seven children; a real surprise. Most of the local law enforcement and fish and game people were there too, as well as the missing park staff. Also present was old

Tom Morris who had recovered from the shock of discovering the murder.

Finally getting his composure, Marty looked at Ranger Nathan and said, "What's the job you wanted me to do?"

Nate said, "Well, for starters, you can cut yonder cake, that is, if any of us are going to eat it."

The party lasted for almost two hours. Marty knew that he had been a hard worker and donated much time, but to be named top volunteer for the entire state was indeed an honor. He had been nominated several times before, so didn't expect this year to be any different. But when it came to a scheduled invitation and flight to the State Capital for a public relations shoot with the Governor, Marty dragged his heels with an emphatic "No!"

Conversation around the room provided favorable circumstances to fill Marty in on all that had happened during his recuperation. "I haven't heard anything about the little blonde headed kid that was camping in the park." Marty started, "What's the latest?"

Nate and Michael relayed the story of the blank film. "His name is supposed to be Nicholas Fix, a fugitive felon from Idaho,"

"Yeah, as ridiculous as it sounds."

"But, he's disappeared," added Michael, "Nobody's seen him since."

Marty also asked about the shower room murder and was told that nothing new had been learned.

"Now, what about all the dead animal life in the pond?" he asked, "What caused it?"

"Toxicology reports have been sequestered and Fish and Game won't tell us a thing," said Nathan, "But they did come and haul off all the dead critters. Whatever it was killed life for almost a mile downstream. Some dogs, cats and a pet duck have been reported so far."

That night, sleep evaded Marty again. Three weeks had passed since the storm and he had more questions and too few answers. Who poisoned the pond, and why? How did the kid relate to the money? Or did he and the murder connect? Where was the kid and was he really a fugitive felon? He had too many angelic attributes to be evil. More than anything, Marty worried about his own sanity. Had he really seen all that money, or did he dream the whole thing? The storm and the falling tree were real enough and so was the two hundred dollars in Marty's wallet.

Somehow he'd have to eventually explain that to Beth. Where in the world did his volunteer vest get to? And what was the subconscious thought that kept evading him? It was a thought he felt would provide many answers. Why was the vision buried in his brain, just beyond his reach?

Chapter Five

Metro Detective Sergeant Anne Lee felt in a panic. The squad room at the 4th Precinct buzzed with unusual activity. Every machine in the room was running and cranking out noise; FAXs and copy machines pushed endless piles of paper. The room, built to hold less than two dozen people comfortably, was jammed with three times that. Uniformed officers and plain-clothes people could not move without bumping into someone else.

"Are all units in place?" Detective Anne was speaking into a red decoder phone. At the other end was Anti-Terrorism's West Coast Commander, retired Admiral James Lincoln. Anne nodded at his affirmative answer and placed the phone back in its cradle.

The room had been converted into a command center for one of the largest sting operations any local agency had ever undertaken.

Loud speakers were droning the communications of four or five different police agencies. The noise was a cacophony of sounds. One wall was covered with electronic boards, maps with moving lights. The lights reflected locations of moving vehicles through the mystery of satellite positioning.

"All units, Stand by!" Anne Lee transmitted simultaneously on all radio frequencies, "Kirkuk is two blocks from ground-zero."

Sgt. Lee was small for a policewoman. She had been clawing her way up the ladder against double prejudice her entire career and was still feeling insecure in a brand new command. She seemed to bristle and was required to force a growl with every command, thinking it to be necessary in order to command respect of her fellow officers who were mostly male.

Activity in the room slowed to a standstill, all voices quiet.

Expectation was high. Tension crackled like high voltage.

The time was 07:43 and 30 seconds on a Sunday morning. It was also New Year's Day.

# # #

Thirty minutes later, Marty and Beth were on the city's most famous landscape known as the Blue Bridge, crossing the river into the heart of the city. Their destination, as on every Sunday was the Morningstar Pentecostal Church. Beth would work in the nursery and Marty would usher during the first service, then they could worship together at the second service. Traffic was lighter than normal for a sunny Sunday morning. The bridge was a wide eight lanes, suspended by gracious cables. It had been patterned after San Francisco's Golden Gate and painted robin's egg blue.

"Something haywire up ahead," Marty said as he began braking to slow their van.

Police barricades were visible and traffic was being turned back on itself. Ten or more blocks beyond the police line a thick oily smoke was hanging low over the downtown part of the city, like a black shroud.

"You'll have to turn around and go back across the river," they were told by an army type Military Policeman.

"What's happening?" Marty asked.

"It's a Homeland Security Incident, now move it, Mac!"

"Can we get across the Steel Bridge?"

"Nope, the whole city center is cordoned off, now get outa' here!"

Heading back to the south side of town, Beth turned on the radio. "Whatever in the world is going on? Can't we get to church?"

"Not unless we drive all the way around to Midvale, fifty-five miles over and fifty-five miles back."

The radio interrupted with that ubiquitous and obnoxious emergency alert tone that has struck terror into the hearts of TV and radio listeners ever since the atomic age unleashed the "Cold War."

After a pulse throbbing pause, the radio intoned, "This is not a drill. The governor has ordered an evacuation of the city center from 48th Avenue to the River. This is not a drill." No reason was given, but the tone and the message repeated over and over.

"Maybe we can get an answer from the TV at home," grumbled Marty.

Matters became worse when they got home, most local stations only showed a test pattern, adding to their stress.

Only one government channel was broadcasting and news came slowly, contradicting whatever was said minutes before. Details were sketchy. Some kind of a terrorist attack had been counteracted by a huge multi level police sting. Only it hadn't been completely thwarted because some kind of "dirty" weapon had been detonated and all of downtown was evacuated.

One announcer said, "Twenty-three people are known dead and the core of the city will be closed for at least five days."

Another announced, "Fortunately there are no injuries, except to the captured perpetrator, and police are even now removing barricades." There had been rumors that the terrorist was from Iraq, but another source listed North Korea. Another suggested Somalia. Nobody was sure about anything.

Speculation was running rampant and the gossip monster grew larger and larger.

Then, they announced for everyone to "Standby for the President of the United States, who would address the Nation in ten minutes."

"I sure want to hear that," said Marty. Just then, the phone rang. It was Nathan. "The park is swarming with Federal Agents," he said, "and they've ordered you to get over here, immediately."

"But... but what's going on?"

"Just get over here, now!" There was a loud click, followed by the dial tone. "But, I want to hear what the President has to say," Marty complained loudly into the dead telephone, knowing that he would not.

I've been a friend of God for a productive 75 years, Marty told himself, *I guess I'm ready to meet my Lord, if this turns out to be as serious as it sounds.* Three times Marty stalled his car on the way to the park. *I'm not nervous, am I?*

When Marty drove in the front gate he was stopped by a Military Policeman, who demanded to see his identification before allowing him to proceed. Other cars trying to enter the park were being turned away.

Questions followed questions. He was only a lowly volunteer so what could they possibly want from him? A chill ran up his spine when he considered that they might already know about the money. With his heart thumping in his throat, Marty parked and entered the main office, hoping for some answers.

The office was a mess. Log books and open files were covering every available surface. Ranger Nathan stuck his head up from out the middle of the mess and said, "Ah, here's the man you want."

He spoke to two others in the room, Detective Sergeant Anne Lee and another very large, slightly balding man that Marty did not know. He had met Anne Lee briefly when she was investigating the dead body in the shower.

"Good morning, Detective," he said. Another chill on the back of his neck and he imagined that he should hold out his wrists. But the expected handcuffs did not appear.

Detective Lee said, "I want you to meet Jim Lincoln from Homeland Security. He has some questions for you."

Lincoln had all the looks of a cop including eyes that seemed to see everything at once. He shifted an annoying bulge under his left arm, and then gave Marty a hefty handshake. Marty grimaced at the pain, but decided this was not a good time to remind this gorilla that he, Marty was a frail old man, instead said, "Can somebody please tell me what's happening downtown?"

"Later." Lincoln replied, "Right now I need some fast answers about the night the tree fell on you." Marty let out a faint breath and slumped slightly forward. Lincoln continued, "What were you doing out on the dike in the middle of such a severe thunderstorm?"

The question was certainly blunt and to the point. Marty hadn't rehearsed any kind of an answer but was able to conjure up an instant reply, without any give-away pause. "One of my dogs was missing and I was looking for her." It was a lie and Marty hoped it didn't show.

Lincoln paused, wrinkled his brow and continued, "Who did you meet?"

"Huh?'

"Don't be difficult. Who did you meet with?" The only human Marty had met outside of routine park visitors was the little kid with the blonde hair, but that had been days earlier.

"Nobody," Marty then remembered the two strangers he had seen while on the ladder. "But I did see two people with flashlights over by the pond."

"Ahah!" Agent Lincoln was interested, "Didn't you challenge them? Ask why they were there?"

"No, they were too far away."

"But, aren't you a sworn employee of the park? Don't you report violations?"

Marty nodded in affirmation. These people were sharp. "Yes, but I'm only a volunteer. It was late and I needed to get home to dry off and warm up." Thinking quickly, he added, "If I hadn't got conked on the head, I would have reported them, but after my coma, I forgot."

"Anyone else?"

"Not that night, but earlier there was this little kid, who the deputy said was wanted for something. Did the police ever find him?"

"No. We don't think he could have anything to do with this," answered Anne Lee. "And he seemed to vanish every time we got a lead on him."

Lincoln seemed satisfied. Softening a bit, he decided to clue Marty in, "Did you know that your night visitors were terrorists? They dumped a mix of strange new viruses and toxins into the pond, waiting for the mess to mature into a new strain of deadly flu. It was intended to be spread by wind and wipe out the whole county. We've caught it in time and have quarantined the area and taken counter measures to stop it. It did however; kill all the fish and ducks.

"Terrorists? From where?"

"We think they are two little known radical splinter groups that have joined forces; one in South America and the other from Indonesia."

"What does that have to do with downtown?" interrupted Ranger Nathan.

"I'll answer that," said Detective Lee, "That was another attempt by the same cell to set off a dirty bomb; they've tried to attack three other cities at the same time. The White House is reporting it now that everything is under control, with minimum damage."

"Can we believe what they say?" Marty blurted it out before thinking. He was answered with silence and smug smiles.

"We've known about this plot for months," continued Anne Lee, "The body in your shower room last month was a Homeland Security Agent who got careless. The bad guys have been here in the park for at least two months, and so have we, undercover. But, we didn't see anything that day. There were apparently no witnesses to pin down who killed the agent."

"The deputies never told us," asked Nathan, "did it happen in the shower, or was the body dragged in there from somewhere else?"

Lincoln gave Nathan and Marty a terse warning. "We're already telling you more than we should, only because of your need to know here in the park, but whatever you've heard here is strictly confidential."

So, the question was never answered, not that it mattered much to Marty and Nathan. Two hours later, all signs of the police and Special Agents were gone, and Nathan and Marty sat in the office alone, staring at each other. Downtown had, in fact, been cleared of non-toxic smoke, barricades had been removed, traffic cleared, and the President's address to the Nation was only a memory. Terrorist Alert Level had been raised again to Orange, but the President convinced everyone that there was no further threat apparent. Events similar had been put down in three other cities.

"Come to think of it," said Nathan, "maybe there was a witness to that murder. Wasn't that on the same night that all the quarters got stolen out of the shower meters?"

"Maybe the police need to know that, too."

"More questions to think about."

Marty said to Nathan, "Neither one of us works on Sundays, why are we sitting here staring at each other? I'm going home. See 'ya tomorrow."

Chapter Six

Marty's conscience bothered him regarding his old friend Tom. Discovering the corpse, followed by hours of police interrogation must have been really hard on the old guy. Tom was ten years Marty's senior and was in the assisted living unit of the retirement home because he suffered from some dementia.

A few weeks after the incident, Marty walked down to the home to see if he could cheer up old Tom with some checkers. They would usually get together at least twice a month. Tom had some short term memory problems, but nothing could interfere with rehashing old fire strategy or unusual rescues the two had been on together. Thirty years of public service generates lots of memories.

"Dispatch calling a phantom box; two - three - two at Fourth and North Main," Marty droned in his best falsetto just outside

Tom's door, "Tenth floor of the Kress building."

From inside the apartment, Tom answered, "Engine 12, Engine 34, Ladder 2 and Squad 1 responding." Opening the door, he added, "Give me a second alarm... Good to see you, Chief."

His wrinkled features and sagging eyes reinforced his ancient look. Instead of mid 80's, he looked more like 105. He wore a faded black sweatshirt emblazoned with the firefighters symbol; a Maltese cross. Most of his teeth were gone. When he reached out to take Marty's hand, his fingers bent beneath large, distorted arthritic knuckles and tears stained his rough weathered face. Tom's eyes seemed soulless, lost in their own torpor.

He always called Marty "Chief", contrary to the fact that Marty had retired with only the rank of Lieutenant, while Tom had been a Battalion Chief. Tom always told Marty that he was going to make it to chief, someday. Marty could have passed the exams for Captain and Chief, but he was satisfied to stay where he was.

Too many things can go wrong in a raging fire situation where top brass were always the scape-goats.

It was unclear whether they would play checkers, go down stairs to the recreation room to shoot billiards, or sit in Tom's room looking at fire department scrapbooks. What they did today would depend on how Tom felt.

"Find any dead bodies today?" asked Marty, tongue in cheek.

"Only one," replied Tom

Taken by surprise, Marty queried, "Yeah? Who?"

"Me!" In spite of his age, Tom never lost his sense of humor. "Gotcha!" he added. "Did they ever I.D. the poor slob in the shower?"

"No, but they're working on it."

"Sit down and tell me about it." They sat for almost an hour and Marty brought Tom up to date on the mystery of the angelic kid and the dead wildlife in the pond. Nothing was said about the money. Marty had also been warned that most of the residents here knew nothing about the terrorist attack on the city, and the administrative psychologist thought it best to keep it that way.

A devilish twinkle spread across Tom's face as he tapped an open scrapbook which he held in his lap. "Remember the Code 99 at the dog tracks?" It was time to reminisce. Marty glanced at his watch.

"Is that the one the *Chronicle's* graphic artist sketched?"

"Yup. Right here in my lap." Marty glanced at the book to refresh his memory. It was a line drawn cartoon of two clumsy firemen carrying old fashioned resuscitation equipment, falling on top of an unsuspecting victim. It had been posted on the front page of the sports section of the *Daily Chronicle*.

"Boy, did he holler!" recalled Marty. The alarm had come in as massive heart attack with the victim passed out on the lawn at the dog races. It was an exceptionally hot day. Marty and Tom were first responders from a station about three miles away. Over by the east gate, they thought they'd located the victim, stretched out in the shade of a tree. Running up to him, Marty's toe got caught in the soft turf and he tripped, falling right in the middle of the 'victim'.

The 'victim' was one of the ticket takers at the gate, taking a break. He was sound asleep in the soft grass, and did he holler.

This would have remained the story of a simple false alarm, nothing more; except it was observed by the Chief Sports Editor of the *Chronicle*, who happened to be watching the races that day. It was funny now, but very embarrassing forty years earlier.

When the talk moved to a time when Marty's brakes went out going down a steep hill driving a 1000 gallon tanker full of water, Marty decided to end the session. "Hey, old timer, I'm late for work. We'll have to finish this later."

Walking back to the park, he felt confident his visit had been a benefit to his old friend. Tom had seen many dead bodies during his career, so the latest one in the park shouldn't cause any long term stress.

# # #

The following week in the State Park was one of boring routine. Only a few hardy visitors came and went. There was no further sign of undercover police. Petty crime however was at a new height for this time of the year. Vandals had been active out on the island. Trail signs were destroyed, map kiosks ripped up, trees cut down to block trails and graffiti carved into benches.

Psychologists have spent eons trying to make sense about why people destroy things that improve life styles. Marty speculated the damage might have been done by poachers who wanted to discourage people and keep the island free of hikers. Nothing else made any sense.

Staff were all aware of the pending lay-offs; moral was down to an all time low. New projects were all on hold, and little work was being accomplished, except the routine, all in anticipation of an unknown and gloomy future. The challenge was gone. Everybody simply existed in 'stand-by' mode.

The shower coin meters had been ripped off again, this time three of them were smashed beyond repair and another shower building had to be closed. Nathan had applied time and time again for a secure token system but the Legislature always vetoed the request as not being "cost effective."

Nathan reported the busted meters and coin theft to law enforcement but they seemed indifferent. They were courteous and took down the information but he was told that Detectives were too busy to be bothered with such trivia.

The weather turned cold and snow could be expected at any time. Most of the regular staff kept busy indoors, sharpening tools, getting snow plows ready, servicing other equipment, taking inventory and doing other support tasks.

The leaves had been raked from the lawn areas, mulched and disposed of and Marty kept busy updating trail maps and hauling rebuilt kiosks to the island to replace the ones vandalized.

He loved every inch of these trails which he had personally carved out of the tangled brush. In the solitude of his work, he would often sing hymns or spend long moments in prayer. Whatever the season, Marty could see God's marvelous hand at work in all the natural things about him.

His work progress was slow because he'd often sidetrack off the trail to visit the lair of a raccoon, the nest of a Red-tail hawk or some other creature. The animals knew him and he had names for many of them. In his reverie, he wondered what ever happened to the chattering Chickaree that had been guarding the money ...oh yes, the money?

In the midst of his praise, that nagging feeling would always return, sending him plummeting from joy to sadness. He knew it was his own guilt convicting him for trying to hide the found money from its rightful owner or from the authorities where it could be an important clue. And, what was that other nagging thought; something he had forgotten; something important that he tried so desperate to remember?

In his meditation, Marty's thoughts were interrupted by a visual disturbance in the soft dirt of the trail. He stared at a fresh, new footprint, but had difficulty focusing. A brief wave of unexpected nausea swept over him, and when it passed he could see that it was the imprint of a small human's shoe, maybe belonging to someone eight or ten years of age.

Then he remembered Nick. *What was his full name?* Ah yes, Nicholas Fix, the angelic looking blonde kid who played war games with lemons and apples.

Happy to abandon the conviction of his conscience, Marty willingly turned his attention elsewhere. *If that danged kid was still here, he'd find him, even if it took all week.* He blinked away a short spell of dizziness and took off following the faint track

# # #

Blood sample #G2552MAB was coded "routine" and as a result, sat on the to-be-tested shelf in the St. Joseph Hospital laboratory for almost two weeks. It had been an unusually heavy testing season what with the advent of Asian Influenza and three new strains of Pneumonia. The lab had been bombarded with rush and urgent samples and had too few staff to handle all of the work. As a result, many of the routine samples for discharged patients had accumulated on the shelves. This was the story behind sample #G2552MAB, which belonged to one Martin Aloyisius Bart.

Lab Technician Mary O'Doul was working alone just before quitting time. She was working catch-up and had processed almost twenty samples since lunch. The lab was so far behind she decided that she could do one more test before shutting down for the day. The sample would be routine and simple, taking less than ten minutes.

Mary was weary after a long day and anxious to be going home to her family. In her fatigue, she could have easily missed the wild indicators.

Something was very wrong with this sample, and she was suddenly fully awake and alert. Her electron microscope was showing a very definite bunya-virus that should not be there.

Further testing revealed enveloped viruses. At ten minutes after five, a cold chill ran down Mary O'Doul's spine. This was deadly serious. There were three single-stranded RNA segments and a very definite indicator of the dreaded *Hantavirus cardiopulmonary syndrome.*

Further testing would be needed, but an alert must be sounded. The patient must be advised immediately.

Mary O'Doul reached for the telephone. "Operator, get me the home of Martin A. Bart, a patient released a week ago Thursday, then I need to make an emergency page for Dr. Rogers."

# # #

Whoever was making the footprints was well versed in concealment. Except for Marty's own outdoor skills, he would have lost the trail completely. Now, all he had to lead him was an occasional snapped twig and a thread caught on a wild rose thorn.
The faint trail seemed to keep turning back on itself. Marty reached a point of confusion, stretching his perseverance.

Another brief wave of dizziness demanded a halt for a brief rest. By now he was tempted with thoughts of giving up the search.

While resting, he scanned the immediate area and there it was!

A little scuff in the bark of a downed log was the last clue, and there, behind the log, he struck pay-dirt!

He saw a two-foot round crawl hole leading into what would appear to be a hut sized pile of brush, overgrown with vines.

Crawling inside, he was amazed at the roominess of the interior. He stood up and looked around. Scrap lumber of various lengths had been engineered into a stable framework. Dead brush and small trees had been bent over the framework to form a thick four sided arbor.

From the inside, the occupant would be able to see in all directions, but not be seen from ten feet outside the perimeter.

Cardboard had been tacked to the inside base in order to help control the wind and to hide any light that might escape from a small propane stove. There were a few clothes hanging from the ceiling, including a boy's size red shirt and on the floor, a rolled up sleeping bag.

Poking around through some trash in one corner, Marty found an old Dinty Moore stew can and the lid to an aerosol insect spray, which he recognized instantly. The shelter had been recently used but there was no sign of the boy.

Marty was certain that he had found the mysterious blond kid's camp. Digging further, he was saddened by a pang of disappointment. For weeks he had secretly wished good things on the lad. He had come to believe the dream that Nick was possibly a supernatural spirit, maybe even an angel. Now that bubble was burst!

Before leaving, Marty brushed the dirt off one piece of damning evidence, a broken piece of hardware that would provide a major piece to the puzzle. He picked it up to be carried out with him, back to Nathan's office. It would answer several questions and be of immense interest to the police. Perhaps Nick really was a wanted fugitive felon.

Marty picked his way out of the area very carefully so as not to tip off the kid that he had been there.

Back at park headquarters, he found that Nathan had gone home early, so he used his key to the office and placed a call to Detective Sgt. Anne Lee. She was out and he left a message.

Then he paged Nathan, who was enroute home in the next county.

"Great news," Marty began, "I've figured out who is ripping off the showers and where the wanted boy is. They're one and the same and I have pretty definite proof."

"What proof?" Nathan's cell phone transmitted.

"The cover and the coin box from one of the busted shower meters."

"Where's the kid?"

"He's very cleverly hidden out on the north island. I've left a message for Sgt. Lee."

"You'll have to lead the search party, you know?" chided Nathan.

"Yeah, I know. I'm not feeling well so I'm headed home. Anne Lee has my home number and I'll call you when I learn what she wants to do."

At home, Marty dropped into his favorite recliner, instantly joined by two happy Shih Tzus. In his fatigue, he failed to notice the flashing message light indicating three calls on the automatic telephone recorder. It had been an exhausting day and he felt very weary. He was asleep within seconds. Beth was out and should waken him when she arrived home.

Marty dreamed that he was very sick. He felt nausea, fever, chills, abdominal and back pain, as well as gastro-intestinal problems. Someone was pounding inside his head loud enough to arouse him into a twilight of wakefulness.

He wanted to yell at his two dogs to get them to stop barking. He then realized the pounding was on his front door. Feeling an icy chill and cold sweat, he rose to answer the door but passed out on the carpet, inches from the door.

Sheriff's deputies and fire department paramedics, who had been called by Dr.

Rogers, forced the door and packed Marty off to the hospital.

# # #

Detective Anne Lee was upset. "We want that kid," she spoke over her shoulder to her partner George Bye, "He's a possible witness, and only Marty Bart knows where he is."

She was holding a telephone, waiting for Dr. Rogers. It was the day after Marty was re-admitted to the hospital. She had received the bad news from Nathan in a telephone call that morning.

A click on the phone preceded a pleasant voice, "Dr. Alice Rogers here."

"Dr. Rogers, this is Detective Anne Lee of Metro, and I need Martin Bart as soon as possible to lead us to a fugitive."

"I'm afraid that is impossible, Detective."

"Why is that?"

"Mr. Bart, Marty, contracted first stage Haemorrhagic Fever with Renal Syndrome, and he'll be bed ridden for three to seven days. It's a form of hantavirus that takes three to five weeks to incubate. It could be fatal if not properly treated. Whatever you want him for will just have to wait. Sorry. Now, if you'll excuse me, I'm due in surgery." It was abrupt and the phone clicked off.

"You get up to the hospital and see if we can at least talk to this old geezer, Anne instructed George. "I'm headed out to the State Park to see what more I can find out."

Driving the five miles out to the park, Anne noticed that it was beginning to snow. She parked at the office and entered, asking the receptionist for Nathan.

"Yes, he's expecting you, go right on in."

In a room off the long hallway to Nathan's office, Anne noticed what looked like a "war-room" with detailed maps of the park and the island which was pierced by numerous colored pins.

Dr. Rogers, it appeared, did not have much esteem for policemen, because Nathan had a wealth of information about Marty's condition, which the good doctor had refused to share with Detective Lee.

"So, tell me," she began, "how can we track this kid down without Marty?"

We've over ten square miles out there," said Nathan, "and all we know is that the boy is camped somewhere in the north end, so that would cut the search area down to maybe four square miles. It would be an impossible task, without more to go on." He escorted her back to the room with the big map in order to emphasize the utter futility of the task.

With a gasp, she said, "I had no idea the area was so huge. Could we get a helicopter in there?"

"Sure. But the trees and brush are so thick, you'd never be able to see a thing."

"Maybe, with the expected snowfall, he might leave tracks?" It was a question and Anne Lee knew that she was out of her element.

"That would appear to be our best option at this time," Nathan replied, "but any searchers will also leave footprints and spook the kid into moving."

"So what do we do next?"

Chapter Seven

Marty was dreaming again. This time, his pain and headaches were gone and he was floating on a fleecy white cloud. He wondered how such a beautiful cloud could be so hot...

It was stifling and he had difficulty breathing. Beth cooled his forehead and stroked his hand, bringing him back to a brief semblance of consciousness.

"Can you hear me, darlin'?" She waited and when she thought she felt a finger twitch, she continued, "Dr. Rogers told me this disease usually runs in five phases. She called them, let me see, I wrote them down: febrile, hypotensive, oliguric, diuretic and convalescent.

She says we caught this in time and that you might jump from phase one directly into phase five. Isn't that good news?"

Marty's cloud was now invaded by a flock of white birds. He felt that they should be called snowbirds, and they were graceful and beautiful. Suddenly each bird regurgitated a green-gray piece of paper. Closer examination revealed the papers to be one hundred dollar bills, and then, the birds turned nasty and attacked Marty, trying to peck his eyes out.

Marty screamed, his fever broke, and he woke up, drenched in a cold sweat.

Beth was out of the room, but Marty's screams brought her and two nurses hurrying back exhibiting signs of panic.

"Welcome back to planet Earth," joked one nurse. "How do you feel?"

Marty groaned and asked for a drink of water. Instead he was poked and probed for all vital signs.

"Do you feel like talking to Detectives?" asked the other nurse, "One has been waiting thirty-six hours to talk with you."

Marty groaned again and managed to get out a weak, "No."

But George Bye, standing in the open door, barged into the room anyway.

# # #

Through the mists and vapors of the half-light dream, Marty knew there was something... some image or something he should be thinking about. What could it be? His vision included his friends in the park, the osprey, the red-tail hawk, the raccoon and the red vixen, along with her two male offspring. Now, how in the world could any of them relate to the missing pieces of Marty's dilemma? Or could they?

Rising up one level of consciousness, he realized that his head hurt. It was that danged detective's fault. George Bye had interrogated Marty to the point of utter exhaustion, and he couldn't even remember what had been asked, let alone what he replied.

Try as he would, the only thing he could remember was Dr. Rogers telling him that he was going to be okay; that his fever had broken and that after a few more days of expected delirium, his head would clear and he would be able to go home.

Then another thought jumped into his consciousness, causing more stress. "The hospital is worried about payment," Beth had told him, "We're only partially covered for these two hospital visits."

"Won't the State pay for the first visit when the tree fell?" It had been a logical question, and the answer surprised everyone.

"State Industrial refused the bill because you were not on duty doing any work for the park, so you're on your own, buddy."

Those words echoed in Marty's brain from words he had heard from Nathan or Michael or somebody..? Marty felt that his whole world was collapsing and something akin to deep depression was setting in.. Beth was in near critical need for medical treatment.

Her nerve and tendon disorders were getting worse, other bills were pressing, and now this!

Beth reassured him with a reminder of God's promise in the Book of Malachi, "It goes something like this," she said, "*If you bring all the tithes into my storehouse, I will pour out a blessing so great you won't have enough room to take it in. Try it! Let me prove it to you.*"

"Yeah," replied Marty, "We've honored God with our full tithe ever since we were married and He has always provided everything we needed. It's just that my faith needs to be stronger. I keep forgetting the basic difference between what we need and what we want."

Marty still dreamed about the lost money. He estimated it close to $50,000 or more, that is, if all the bills in the three packets were the same denomination. It was too bad he had never had a chance to count it. Portraits of Benjamin Franklin on America's "C" Note currency haunted his every thought. His brain was in conflict.

Holy Scripture often jumped into his thinking to convict him, and he knew that he had a moral responsibility to tell the police about the money, but so far, could not bring himself to surrender.

A verse from Proverbs 20, memorized as a child, kept repeating over and over: *"Bread of deceit is sweet to a man; but afterwards his mouth shall be filled with gravel."* (vs. 17).

Police had been stationed in the hallway outside Marty's hospital room, like he was a criminal awaiting trial. Beth complained bitterly about it, but the detectives would not relent.

"If Marty doesn't come out of his delirium soon, the kid is going to move again," said Detective Lee, "and we'll never find him."

George reminded her, "I've got enlarged maps of the island down in the car, just waiting for him to recover."

"Why is he so important to you?" asked Beth. "You weren't at all interested in him last month."

"We're pretty sure now that he knows something about the agent that was murdered in the shower room. He's not a suspect but maybe witnessed it," said Anne Lee.

Marty's eyes were closed, but his brain was wide awake and he heard all this. That is when he decided to quit "playing possum" and respond to their needs. "I'm awake," he said, and it hit the room like a thunderbolt.

George Bye was out the door in a flash and returned a minute later with a large roll of maps. Meanwhile, after checking pulse and blood pressure, the nurse had propped Marty up in the bed.

He was surprised how good he felt. "I feel euphoric. Let me try standing," he pleaded.

"Not until the doctor has a good look at you," replied the nurse.

George edged in between them with his maps. Marty had a little difficulty focusing, but after studying a bit, was able to pin the search area down to a little less than two square miles.

"It was right around here, someplace," he said, pointing to the paper, "Without actually seeing the trail, the trees and other natural features, I can't really tell."

"That still leaves us nowhere," growled George, as he stormed out.

Marty was left alone for a few hours and tried to sleep, but thoughts of the murder, the boy and the money kept creeping in and agitating his thoughts. He couldn't decide if he wanted to help the police locate the boy or not. The more police activity in the park, the more it would interfere into his personal efforts to locate the missing cash. Each time he fell asleep, he startled back into wakefulness, reaching for that elusive image that hovered just outside his range of vision

Chapter Eight

In a downtown hotel room, across the river and miles away from Marty's hospital, two men of Eastern descent were in a heated discussion.

Albusi Mahk ran course fingers through his fine black beard, combing out the remaining crumbs from his lunch. "So the Infidels neutralized the pond, also?" He was speaking to his chief weapons of mass destruction technician. "You have failed twice," He continued threateningly, "By the gods, once more and you will cease to exist."

Hakim al-Awi bowed and backed out of the room. He was a tiny, wiry sort of a man. Weapons of mass destruction had been his lifelong study. In spite of the stigma attached to his profession, he was a kind and thoughtful main stream Muslim. He had serious doubts about the terrorist cells he was working with; their goals and warped ideals left him with many questions.

The harsh words bounced off Hakim's tender skin, like a stinging slap across the face. It was the worst of all the other abuse he daily received from Albusi Mahk and his cronies. Hakim had done his job well; it was Mahk who had allowed the element of surprise to be thwarted. Self respect and self pride are high on every Muslim's list of attributes. Attacking them was as severe as a blade between the ribs. Today's sting of rebuttal remained as he shuffled back to his quarters and he inwardly seethed with a festering fantasy of revenge.

# # #

For two weeks, Hakim's rage putrefied, but he was a patient man, knowing how to wait for perfect opportunities. He kept busy studying which helped to pass the time. He knew that Mahk had imminent plans for more terrorism. *But why was he waiting so long?*

On Tuesday, he was listening intently to the sounds drifting up from the street below. He was nervous and suspicious of every unusual sound, as any fugitive from justice would be. A mere pin drop in the hallway outside his cheap hotel room would result in panic. He wasn't sure just who he feared most: his cell-chief, Albusi Mahk, or Federal agents, or average citizens who hated Muslims in general.

It was Hakim's brother who had died trying to set off the "dirty-bomb" weeks earlier. That scare had evacuated much of the city core, but when the officials allowed people to return, Hakim figured this downtown place to be the safest for him to hide, just across the street from the burned out shell of a building where his brother died.

By now, he figured, the authorities would have been able to place a name on his brother's few grizzled remains and so, be looking for him as well. He was seriously considering flight away from the entire mess, when his cell phone tone alerted him back to reality.

Chapter Nine

Later the next day, Dr. Rogers released Marty to go home and with a good bill of health. She would not allow any outdoor activity for at least 24 hours. The detectives relented at the inconvenience and scheduled Marty to meet them at the park office at noon the following day.

Much to Marty's objection, Beth insisted on driving him over to the park the next day and she insisted he use a cane when walking.

"Grumble all you want," she said, "Dr. Rogers says you'll still have dizzy spells and need help keeping your balance. Marty knew he could not win this argument.

Nathan's map room was a hub of activity when they arrived. Three police officers were busy stretching string between pins to triangulate something; it wasn't quite clear what. A more relaxed George Bye met Marty there, triggering instant suspicion. "Ready to go?" he asked politely, "I have a surprise for you."

Outside, George led the way to a fleet of three little John Deere gasoline scooters called "gators". Each had an enclosed cab and comfortable seats for two people. "We'll use these until we run out of trail," he said, "that should make it easier on your recovery."

The little caravan of gators made its way along the flood control dike toward the island. Rocks in the dike surface made the little vehicles buck and bounce until Marty groaned, complained of vertigo and requested a slower speed. When he regained composure, he spoke with George about Nick Fix, the angelic boy fugitive.

"You know, he told me he was 13," said Marty, "but I swear he looks only 8 or 9. Why is he wanted in Idaho?"

"They say that he's a runaway and that he shoplifted something large enough to make him a felon," replied George.

"What do you mean, large enough?"

"Theft is usually a misdemeanor, but when the value exceeds $250, it becomes a felony."

"What did he steal?"

"Some kind of jewelry, I heard."

Geez, Marty thought, *Now my little cherub is an international jewel thief.* The absolute stupidity of the charge reminded him of Peter Sellers in the "Pink Panther" series. *Too funny.* And he chuckled out loud.

Accompanied by four plainclothes policemen in the two other gators, they drove down off the dike and started out the crossing trail to the island. The water in the channel separating the island from the mainland was an average four inches deep and about a hundred yards across.

Several Great-blue herons launched with a horrible screech, as the little caravan came out of the trees and splashed into the water. Schools of tiny trout fry fled in all directions at the intrusion.

The gators drove through it easily, except that George failed to navigate around some of the creek boulders, causing sufficient lurch which wrenched Marty's neck and made his headaches return. He was grateful for their return under the dense

95

canopy of shade trees and to a smoother trail.

In the lead gator, George Bye startled and suddenly stopped as something bounded across the trail ahead of him.

"Wha.. what the devil was that?" he asked.

Marty laughed and said, "One of the many feral animals that live out here. People abandon pets that turn wild. That was a pot-bellied pig we've been trying to catch for over a year. You wouldn't think that a pig could move that fast, the noisy gators frightened it. I'm surprised that our boy, Nick hasn't had him for dinner." Marty drew a deep breath and continued, "You know, he's going to hear these gators coming, from a mile off."

Not long after that, they parked the gators and continued on foot. Marty warned them to walk silently, but the city cops didn't know how. They seemed to stomp on every dry twig, sounding an audible alarm a mile ahead of them. Then he suggested that they wait while he continued on alone, but they would have no part of that, either.

"We're out here to haul him in for questioning," replied George, "not to play Daniel Boone stalking the Indians."

"Whatever you say," replied Marty, knowing full well on this day, they would never see their quarry.

As predicted, their quest came to an abrupt stop when Marty led them up to the hidden vine enclosure, empty of all belongings. Marty could tell that the kid had only vacated minutes before. He felt the ground and noted slight heat where the propane stove had been in use, but figured it would be useless to try to tell these city cops anything. In their disappointment and anger, they wouldn't have listened anyway.

Marty was weary and glad for the chance to ride home in one of the gators. He had an idea about the boy, but didn't share it with the detectives. It was an idea that he would check out later, on his own.

# # #

Reginald Fix was plotting his defense while sitting in the Kootenai County jail awaiting trial for conspiracy to commit grand larceny. He felt that the stupid attorney the county had assigned him didn't know his law from his jaw. The dummy had told him, "You do the crime, you do the time." What kind of a stupid defense was that? Reginald knew that he would have to have better counsel.

Reginald was one of those career criminals with a rap sheet in eight different western states. He felt that the cops were too dumb to put his history together, because he felt jurisdictional pride would prohibit agencies from communicating with each other.

He couldn't have been more wrong. Right now, he had been picked up relative to casing out an armored car at a Federal Reserve bank. He didn't know it, but one of his co-conspirators had spilled the beans, and all five would-be bandits were being held in five different jails.

He also didn't realize that the Feds had combined his many rap sheets and warrants from all state jurisdictions into one federal indictment.

"Wake up, Reggie," called a Corrections Officer, "you've got visitors."

"Yeah?"

"Hop to it! They're feds from Homeland Security."

One slipper on, and one lost, he was hustled into a private interrogation room where two beefy investigators were waiting.

They frowned and Reginald's heart missed a beat. Their first question took him completely by surprise,

"What did you do to make your little brother, Nicholas run away?"

"You have Nick? Where's Nick?"

"You tell us. Answer the question."

"He just ran away because he missed his ma and he couldn't make it at school." It was a lie and Reginald knew it.

"Ya gotta do better than that!" growled one of the agents.

"We haven't got all day," said another.

"Well. ugh..ah..ah..." One agent began to apply pressure to his elbow joint,

"Ow, that hurts! I don't know 'nuthin." Three times in an hour, they jousted back and forth, until Reginald Fix finally wore down.

"The truth, Reggie!"

"Some friends of mine stole a diamond broach and I set him up to take the blame. After his mother died, the State took over her house and he had no place to go..." Reginald continued with his confession, while one of the agents made a phone call.

"Just like we thought," he said, "the kid is innocent." Admiral James Lincoln was on the other end of the conversation.

"Get word to the city detectives."

# # #

The next morning, Marty and Beth were sitting at their breakfast nook, over two cups of mocha.

"What are we going to do about the bills," Beth was serious.

"Like we always have done, honey," said Marty, "We trust in the Lord. He's always come through for us, there's no reason to deny Him now." He took a sip of his mocha and continued, "I do have a little confession and a small surprise for you." He reached for his wallet and laid the two one-hundred dollar bills on the table before her.

Beth's eyes widened and she exclaimed, "Where in the world...?"

Marty told her about the two bills and the first one that he had already used to pay debts. "I knew that I would be telling you sooner or later." he said meekly, and then added, "There was a whole lot more where this came from, but I've lost it."

After a sob or two, he told her the whole story. "So you see," he concluded, "I wasn't in the park that night of the storm looking for Me Tzu. Instead, I was picking up the money."

They sat in silence for a moment; Beth absorbing. Marty watched her face for a sign of what she was feeling. He knew that he felt a lot better; like a huge weight had been removed from his shoulders.

Beth broke the silence and said, "It just disappeared, just like that young boy you told me about. Do you suppose there's connection?"

"I don't know," Marty replied, "but I've been fighting my conscience for weeks. I'm glad that I've finally told somebody."

"I'm more than just somebody, dear," she whispered, "I'm your wife and best friend."

"I'll have to tell the police and Nathan about the money," Marty said, "And it will be a huge load off my mind. The money has to connect to some of the crap that's been happening around here lately."

They sat for awhile longer in silence, and then Marty got up to leave. "I don't think I'll go to work today," he said, "I'll be in the park, but doing something else. I've got an idea where the kid might be."

Marty checked in with Nathan at the park office. "Hi there mean old boss," he said. It was a joke they had between them as Nathan was neither mean nor old. "I don't feel well enough to work, yet, "he continued, "so I'll just walk around some and enjoy the trails for awhile. Is there anything new on the investigations?"

"Glad you stopped by," Nathan said," Detective Lee just called. She said that the Feds have cleared your boy, Nick. He's still wanted for questioning, but the felony fugitive warrants have been canceled. But we still have to settle the question about the park's shower meters. Your intuition was right about him the whole time."

"Great," replied Marty, as he walked out, still using the cane that Beth had provided. It was an exceptionally bright sunny day for January, but extremely cold.

Marty strolled over to the back side of the juvenile fishing pond. It was frozen, possibly thick enough for ice-skating, but the Parks Commission had recently suggested a prohibition, probably because they couldn't afford the liability. Signs had been posted, but some brave folks still skated. It would be a pleasure to sit and daydream again about his beautiful Beth sliding so gracefully on the ice, twirling like a ballerina. Daydreams came easily the older he got, but right now, he had an idea that had to be checked out.

He sat for a long time on a stump, trying to piece together a puzzle that had been annoying him. After awhile, he got up and headed straight into a tangle of brush and berry vines. There was another huge cluster of dead brush and small trees that formed a natural arbor, just like the one out on the island. Marty remembered seeing this one from the previous year, and sure enough, there it was! Many of the saplings and vines had been pulled together and held with brush colored twine. Three sides of this hut were hidden by impenetrable masses of blackberry canes, the only observation side being straight out to the iced-over fishing pond and everything beyond. It was a perfect hiding place. Inside, he found the familiar red shirt, sleeping bag, the long missing mystery fishing pole and other property. There was an old partly broken patio chair, one leg propped up by a piece of firewood, and Marty settled himself into it, preparing for a long wait.

Sitting in the broken chair wrapped in a warm coat, he allowed himself to doze, knowing that he would hear if anyone should approach.

After awhile, he heard a faint shuffle of pebbles rolling under foot and was instantly alert. The kid climbed into the enclosure and while his eyes adjusted to the dark interior, Marty moved swiftly to the entrance to block any attempt to flee.

"Hello, my friend Nick," he said, "I'm here to help."

Nick blinked, glanced at Marty and said, "I am so busted!"

"You are not in trouble, my friend, you are saved. Let's sit here awhile and talk." The first thing Marty told him was that his older brother Reginald had confessed to setting him up for the jewelry heist and that he didn't have to live out here hiding from people anymore.

"What about the money I stole from the showers?"

"I'll pay for that," said Marty.

"Why?"

"Because I think you're a good kid and I like you. The only thing you need is a little love. He could see a new twinkle in the kid's overly blue eyes and muscles in his neck and hands begin to relax a little. A slight smile begin to appear on his angelic face. "You look like you haven't had a decent meal in weeks,"

Marty suggested, "Wanna go home with me for a good hot meal? Marty fished around in his pockets to produce a Granola bar which Nick eagerly accepted.

They talked on for almost an hour. Marty explained why the police wanted to talk to Nick, assuming he had witnessed the murder. To his surprise, Nick admitted he had and that he really wanted to tell somebody about it.

"I was in the next shower stall, ripping off the quarters, when a man entered to pee. Then another man with a big black beard sneaked in behind him and strangled him with a taught wire around the neck. It was awful..."

Marty interrupted, "Don't tell me anymore, but will you talk to the police?"

"Sure, as long as I don't have to go to jail or something."

Marty helped him gather up his few belongings, then stopped briefly at the park office to tell Nathan the boy had been found and that Marty was taking him home to have Beth put some tender loving care (and some food) into him.

Beth received Nick like he was her long lost son. Marty and Beth had seven children, but they were all grown up, married and moved across the country. They all acted like most kids of the era, keeping involved in their own lives and seldom calling or writing to a family who cared deeply for them.

Their failure to understand the separation hurt Beth and Marty deeply.

The police finished with Nick, who identified Albusi Mahk from rogue's gallery photos as being the killer of the Homeland Security agent, and a nationwide search was underway for the fugitive terrorist. The police had no doubt because Nick described every detail of the murder, including the stripping off of the victim's clothing and the sadistic way he was propped up in the shower stall.

Nathan, Marty and Nick were glad to have the police out of their lives and out of the park. If there was ever a trial, Nick would be called to testify, but just to be safe, Anne Lee video-taped his deposition.

Beth doted on Nick and Marty took him to work in the park with him every day. Ranger Nathan decided there would be no charges filed for the broken shower meters, as long as Nick agreed to do some community service in the park under Marty's supervision. Nick was most happy with this arrangement.

Marty and Nick were two of a kind insofar as their love and understanding of Nature. It answered Marty's most pressing question when he learned Nick's tracking and woodsman skills were real, explaining much of his ability to quickly appear or to suddenly vanish like magic. Nick knew all about the red fox vixen and the other creatures that Marty loved. The two worked well together; like a finely oiled timepiece. It thrilled all they came in contact with, to see such a vaporized generation gap.

Chapter Ten

Driving north into the park, Hakim was thinking about home and his squalid childhood. His motivation to join the insurgency had been motivated primarily by poverty and reinforced by boredom. The money and better lifestyle were always desired.

Now, at last, he was wealthy beyond his wildest dream, but still bored. Life held no apparent promise; no future, no hope. His family had all been killed in one of the many civil conflicts. His lonesome despair was another reason for joining a "family" of insurgents, like a kid joins a street gang when real love is denied him at home.

He was not really a bad guy, just a disillusioned puppet and a good devout Muslim. He believed the idea of *Jihad* warfare and martyrdom was carried much further than ever envisioned by the writers of the *Qur'an*.

As he pulled into the State Park, his thoughts were still in far away Egypt, and he was unaware of his excessive speed.

Assistant Ranger Dave Scott was on duty because it was Nathan's day off. Dave had been gone for three months to Ranger School at the state capitol, and today was his first day back on the job.

His plan for the day was to catch up by reading the activity logs and new directives. It would be a boring day stuck in the office when he'd rather be outdoors on such a beautiful sunny winter day. Dave checked in with Angie, the front desk receptionist, then headed for his office, fully expecting a wearisome, monotonous day.

Before he could open the first directive, the sound of a badly tuned Trans-Am roared past the office.

"I'd guess forty-five miles per hour," said Angie, as Dave ran past her and out the door to his enforcement vehicle. Maximum speed anywhere in the park was ten miles an hour and was strictly enforced.

Blue lights ablaze, Dave closed on the black Trans-Am almost a mile from the park entrance. The car pulled into a parking space near the fishing pond.

Standing slightly behind the door frame, as law enforcement teaches for bodily protection, Dave asked for a driver's license, "Do you know that you were driving thirty miles over the speed limit?"

"I left my license in other pants," pleaded Hakim. Then, defensively, "Where are speed limit signs?"

Dave thought, *This guy is either blind or stupid,* replying, "It's well posted, sir."

"You give ticket?"

"A warning citation, only, this time." said Dave, "What's your name?"

Hakim's fear led to belligerence, "Bah! You only Ranger. I don' have to take you damn ticket." At that, he floored the Trans Am and headed back out of the park at a high rate of speed.

Rather than pursue the fleeing vehicle, Ranger Dave radioed the State Police to run the vehicle license. It turned out to be stolen, and Dave left the matter in the hands of the Troopers.

Marty and Nick had been applying stain to a dumpster pad fence only a few yards away and walked over to talk with Dave. "What was that all about?" asked Marty.

"The State Troopers will nail him," said Dave, I have no idea who he was or what he wanted, but the car was stolen."

"I've seen him in the park several times,' added Nick, "He was with that black bearded guy that murdered the man in the shower."

"Did you mention him to the police?" asked Dave.

"No, I forgot all about him until just now."

"Well, something appears to be coming down," said Dave. "Both of you get in the truck. We've got to call Homeland Security; they'll sure want to talk to one or both of you."

Back at the office, the call made, Dave went back to his studies while Marty and Nick settled down to a game of gin-rummy while waiting for the Federal agents. Angie brought coffee for Marty and Hot Cocoa for Nick.

"What's floating in the cocoa?" Nick was serious.

Angie winked at him, "It's only a marshmallow, silly." Angie had two boys of her own and had taken a special liking to Nick. She continued, "It's time you were introduced to some of the little pleasures of life."

When two agents arrived from Homeland Security, they determined a need to transport Nick downtown for some pretty intense questioning. Marty volunteered to go along with him and the Feds did not object.

"Take the gin-rummy cards with you," hollered Angie as they started out the door, "Police stations are notorious for 'hurry-up-and-wait'."

# # #

Hakim al Awi was frightened. He knew they would report him and that he was busted. He realized that his panic in the park had been a major mistake, but at this point he really didn't care. It was the final straw; the excuse he was looking for; it was all he needed to conclude his parting from the terrorists. He would not return to Albusi Mahk, whose only solution to failure was assassination. So that left him on the run with no place safe to go.

He would not panic again. Islamic background had taught him one valuable lesson. A pause and a deep slow breath restored a clear mind, and a cool logic swept over his entire being; his instinct for survival kicked in and he suddenly had a plan.

There was an unused and brush choked lane that used to service old man Jacobs homestead. Punch Jacobs was the cranky horse-breeder who pastured his horses next door to the park. Hakim al Awi knew that Jacobs no longer lived on the property because he had made too many threats with his shotgun to State Park visitors who accidentally trespassed on his pasture.

Nathan had filed charges and the Judge had given Jacobs the option to surrender the shotgun or to move. The old man chose the latter. It was a perfect place for Hakim to hide. The last place officials would look for him was in or around the State Park.

He chuckled as he thought about the next step he would take. It was ingenious! Flipping open a non-traceable cell phone, he dialed 9-1-1.

"Tell Homeland Security that terrorists plan to dump another canister of toxins in the State Park, tonight."

"Who is this? ... Hello? ..." The operator heard only a dial tone. And Hakim wore a smile you could see a mile. For the first time in his life, he felt like he was in charge.

# # #

Nick's interrogation was routine and straight forward. It was accepted that he had actually forgotten Hakim's presence at the murder.

The agents were not able to extract any evidence to support a case of accomplice to murder or conspiracy against Hakim. He could be taken in for nothing stronger than a witness to murder.

Marty and Nick had been separated and both questioned by different agents, and after a couple hours and some sworn statements, were free to go.

Marty's conscience had dictated an earlier confession to the police about finding the money, but they insisted that it had nothing to do with any of the current investigations. So far as officialdom was concerned, the money was only a myth; a figment of Marty's imagination.

"If it ever shows up again," Detective Sergeant Anne Lee laughed, "It is yours to keep and enjoy."

"Great," Marty exclaimed sarcastically, "It really was there, and I'm going to find it! But, only where?"

Nick, overheard this exchange and whispered into Marty's ear, "Tell me about it. Maybe I can help."

Marty looked at him through questioning slanted eyes, "I know that you know how to move without trace through the woods and vanish like a wraith, and that you see lots of things that nobody else sees, but little buddy, you wouldn't be holding out something on me, would you?" Marty wasn't sure why he was suddenly suspicious.

Nick answered with a sly smile that more closely resembled a smirk. "Time will tell," he stated, "I think I have an idea."

Chapter Eleven

"Peen" Hatchet leafed through the latest issue of *Skinhead Magazine*. His reading skills were limited and he was more interested in pictures, especially if they were comfort pictures suggesting food, alcohol, sex or other pleasures. The truth was he was bored, and wanted some action.

Jason Hatchet had carried the nickname "Peen" ever since his initiation into a Neo-Nazi chapter known as the "Dusty Panthers." Peen stood for the ball-peen hammer that he used to bash the skull of a person of color ten years earlier in Arkansas. It had been a required part of his gang acceptance.

On this day, he was confined to his old Volkswagen van, following orders to do surveillance in the State Park. His Chapter had written a "bill of termination" (A contract) on certain Muslims that had been seen in the area. Hate crimes were their passion.

Peen yawned. He had been watching people in the park for three hours, and he was tired. Tired of laughter and happy people; tired of people enjoying themselves and having fun; maybe he was tired of something else, like trying to figure out why they were so happy and he was not.

When Black or Yellow children played together with the Whites, it made the skin on the back of his neck crawl. *How could they get along so well together? They must be sick!*

What he didn't realize was that more than ten of the "white" children in the playground were from a nearby Lebanese Mosque School and their parents looked like any other Caucasian.

Muslims were invisible right in front of him, but his prejudice continued to play tricks on him and his conscience.

"Wake Up, Leo!" he called over his shoulder to a sleeping figure in the back of the van. "Ain't no damned Muslims here today and I need to take a break."

Leo ("the Lizard") Leonart groaned at the interruption, and began to stir.

"We gotta get outa here," Peen continued, "The damned Ranger has been by three times eyeballing us, and the last time by, he wrote down my license number."

"So," answered Leo, "You've still got a stolen plate on it, don't you?"

"Yeah, and it's time to change it again, maybe to Wisconsin" said Peen, as he drove out of the park.

The Dusty Panthers headquartered in an abandoned railroad switchman's tower in the middle of the Ogden and SantaFe rail yard. Freight was moving on all sides and their hideout was ideally secluded. The only access was by way of a tunnel that passed under fifteen busy switching tracks. It was a bit noisy, but served their purpose well.

Bunks and a makeshift kitchen filled the first two windowless stories. One battery operated black & white TV, a gasoline Coleman lantern and a three-burner propane stove were the only signs of civilization.

The place stank of urine, unwashed bodies, booze and vomit, masked under a sickly smelling floral deodorant. The members who slept there had been conditioned so long to the foul odors that no one noticed them anymore.

A barn owl family and a hundred pigeons occupied the third floor, where the switchman used to sit. Trains now ran by computer control and manual switching was no longer necessary.

All the upper windows had long been broken out, and the place had been stripped of all copper wire and anything else of value.

It was evening when Peen and Leo arrived; not that one could tell night from day when inside. They found the place in an uproar. Some ten other chapter members were in heated discussion about a series of gangland type killings that were in the news.

"The Red Norteños have always been friendly to us," growled one tough, "And they've asked for our help."

Peering through the blue haze of marijuana smoke, Peen interrupted the speaker. "What's coming down?"

"Sureños Blues are on the warpath, gathering forces from down south," explained another, "They claim the Reds screwed them out of fifty big ones in a sour drug deal, last month. One of them stashed the money in a tree somewhere and then got blasted. None of the other Blues know where the tree is."

"I say we keep out of it," said a husky man who appeared to be a leader.

"I second that," said Peen." The matter was heatedly discussed, voted and dropped, at least for the present.

# # #

Nathan called an urgent meeting of his entire staff. This was the scheduled day when even the summertime part-time aides were ordered to attend.

When Marty arrived with another volunteer, almost all the paid staff members were already there, sitting around the huge table in the conference building. They were instantly aware of the gloom and doom expressions visible on many faces. The air was full of static, thick as the air in a smoky tavern.

Marty recalled the last time he was in this room, a time of gladness and pleasure; the celebration of his Volunteer of the Year award. What a contrast to this mandatory meeting.

As the last of staff filed in and found seats, Nathan rose and cleared his throat, "I think most of you know why this sad meeting is being called." He paused, looking around the room. It was obvious that he had trouble making eye contact with anyone. His dry voice sounded an octave higher than usual, revealing his distress. A hush of expectation fell over the room. The figurative lightning was poised to strike momentarily.

"I have to get through this, quickly, before I bawl," said Nathan. "I love each and every one of you. You've been my right hand and have helped make our park one of the best destination parks in the state, if not the very best!" A red kerchief appeared in his hand to dab the corner of an eye. "Six Aides of the lowest seniority have already been given thirty-day notice. You all know who you are."

One of the Aides asked, "Is there any chance the Legislature will restore some or all of our funding?"

"There's always a chance, but right now, the prospects look pretty slim." Nathan paused in obvious distress then took a deep breath and added, "With God, all things are possible."

Assistant Ranger Dave Scott stood up, "Let me help you out, Nate." After a short pause, he continued, "Camp circles K, L and M will be closed effective immediately along with both boat ramps. We will lock the gates to two of the playgrounds and one tennis court. Mowing will cease in Section G and be allowed to return to meadow. The Maintenance crews gets cut in half, and you already know who leaves and who stays. That leaves the question of the Ranger Trainees..."

"I'll speak on that," interrupted Nathan. "Thank you! As Dave said, it's a sticky question. All six trainees came on at the same time, so seniority can't decide which three stay and who will have to go. Headquarters has approved the use of a chance lottery to decide. This is what I have done: Six sealed envelopes contain the six Trainee names in this hat." He picked up a ranger's campaign hat and placed it on the table beside him.

"Six more envelopes contain a one word message. Three of them say 'Layoff' and three say 'Stay'." He spread six more sealed white envelopes on the table.

"Angie, our receptionist, will pick an envelope out of the hat, open it and announce the name. That Trainee will then randomly choose one of the message envelopes, but not open it until all the envelopes are gone. Fair enough?" The best I can do for three unlucky people, will be to help file for Unemployment insurance."

People around the room nodded their assent. Later, when the meeting adjourned, eleven staff members had to take news of termination home to their families. The politics of running a government had again achieved lop-sidedness. Somebody's 'pork' was more important than the lives of honest laboring taxpayers.

Marty agreed with all the others, that the State government was misguided, deceived and just plain wrong. Parks and Recreation had always been at the bottom of the budget brouhaha, but this action would create destruction that could never be repaired.

If the Legislature wanted chaos they would get it.

The meeting ended with sad good-byes. Friendships had been formed and would last forever, but careers ended abruptly.

Two of the laid-off aides did promise to stick around as unpaid volunteers; probably the only 'good' to come out of the day, if that could be called, good.

Afterwards, Nathan, Dave and Michael were left alone in the big room; the only paid employees remaining to finish out the winter and spring seasons. After Memorial Day a few temps would return but so would thousands of campers. The three stared at

each other in silence, knowing there was no way the park could maintain any degree of standard. So much more would now depend on the volunteers.

# # #

Marty and Nick were spending more and more time communing with the natural heartbeat of the 'Island'. The weather was beginning to warm and flood waters were rising. Soon, the many arroyo channels would begin filling with backwater, predictable as the higher elevation snow melt raised levels of the local rivers.

With the impending layoffs, Nathan was putting more and more pressure on his few volunteers. But Marty ignored his pleas and Nathan knew why. Years before, when Nathan was first promoted to Head Ranger, they had made an oral agreement.

"I'll work hard for you summer, fall and winter, but springtime is my time," Marty told him. And Nathan agreed.

And, indeed by mid February, spring was early. Marty was showing Nick the tiniest and earliest spring blossom, that of the wild Hazelnut, also known as a Filbert. Also blooming early were Salmonberry and Wild Ginger, both hardly noticeable; the one several feet above a hiker's ordinary vision line, the other hidden under the molding leaf duff. Little mounds of the previous year's rotting leaves were being pushed up like miniature volcanoes by new fern fiddleheads and trilliums.

Standing very very still, they could hear the faint rustle of dried leaves as moles and mice tunneled beneath them. .Areas open to full sun would soon be ablaze with yellow violets, often called Johnny jump-ups. It was a magic time for Marty and Nick.

"Listen," said Nick, "Hear that?" A new sound echoed in their ears, ever so faintly.

"Redwings have returned," answered Marty. "The pond reeds are alive with them."

Nick turned his nose into the faint breeze, and sniffed. He had been blessed with super acute senses and sharpened them further with an outstanding outdoorsman's skill. "We've got company," he announced, "about two hundred yards toward the river. It's a man and probably a poacher."

Astonished, Marty asked, "How do you know he is a poacher?"

"I can smell him."

"Sweat?"

"No, it's a mixture of after-shave lotion, beer, cigarette smoke and fish guts," said Nick, "Fishing season is still two months away. Shall we go get him?"

Marty thought for a second before replying, "We're not on duty, we have no park insignia and no radio or cell phone to call for back-up. We can try to spy him out, but it's not wise to approach him, or to let him see us."

An aging and slower old man and a spry eight-year old now blended their tracking skills. They crept silently and unseen toward the river in a way to elicit pride from any Apache or Ogalala Sioux. A very unsuspecting individual sat on the river bank, casting with a hand fishing line. He was small for a man. At his side was an empty pony case of Budweiser beer along with two very nice trout.

A mere twelve feet behind the man, Marty and Nick lay hidden in the brush. The two woodsmen glanced at each other, and both nodded. Marty motioned retreat and man and boy vanished like wraiths. The fisherman had no clue that he had been observed.

"No question about it," whispered Nick when they were far enough away to talk without being heard. "He's the Muslim the cops are looking for; what's his name?"

"Hakim al-Awi," said Marty. "I think he might be camped out here somewhere."

"Why do you think that?

"He's fishing in order to eat, not for the sport of it."

"Should we tell the police?" asked Nick.

"Not yet," said Marty, "Let's stake him out and see where he goes, first."

# # #

The Emergency Communications Operations Center for the city had been consolidated with the county and three other nearby communities. A year earlier, they combined fire; police and emergency medical response into one finely knit organization and rewarded themselves with a new building and the latest in technology. All 9-1-1 calls were filtered through this center before being handed off to appropriate agencies. Fire, police and EMS dispatchers were also located in adjoining parts of this same room. The Center served approximately three million people. All telephone and radio traffic was constantly recorded by sophisticated digital equipment.

Adrianne Grenlach, Shift Supervisor placed an urgent call to her electronics shop manager, Joe Amicarilli.

"Hi, Joe! Any luck with that State Park Arabian accent call? Homeland Security is pushing me for the tape."

"It was an unlisted cell phone, but satellite pinned it down to have originated in the park."

"How are you coming with the voice comparisons?"

"Good enough to stand up in a Court of law," said Joe, then adding, "If we only had a suspect."

"You might as well bring the tape up here because they're on the way here to pick it up for transport to the Federal forensics lab in Dallas." She hung up to take another call.

It was her old friend Detective Sergeant Anne Lee. They had been Academy rookies together.

Anne Lee had a special request and information to exchange relating to the investigation of a recent gangland type triple murder. The media had been covering nothing else for the past two days.

The murders set off a domino effect which now involved Neo-Nazis and the dominant north and south gangs. A major rumble was being threatened and Anne wanted Adrianne to be forewarned.

"We still haven't caught the terrorists, either," concluded Anne. "The whole county is going to hell in a hand basket."

"Can you tell me anything about what caused the three murders?" asked Adrianne.

"It was actually four," said Anne, "And we've had a good laugh about the cause. It's still confidential but I don't mind telling you."

"I heard something about a drug deal gone bad," offered Adrianne

"Right. A Sureño gang boss set up a big meth sale with an unknown John Doe who was supposed to stash his money somewhere in the woods, but before delivery could be made, a splinter group of skinheads attacked and killed our John Doe, who is still down in the morgue. He happens to be a Muslim, so we can guess the motive for the first murder to be an unrelated racial hate crime.

"The gang leader knew where the money was supposed to be, but on the way to pick it up, got into a bloody fight with some Norteño Reds and got blasted. We recovered the meth and two bodies, but nobody knows where the money is. The other two murders were in retaliation. Word on the street is that the Dusty Panthers have been asked to help out the Red Norteños."

"I hope they all wipe each other out," said Adrianne. "So now it sounds like open war, heh?"

"Right," said Ann, "I just thought you'd like to know."

"Now, I've got a tip for you," said Adrianne. "The 9-1-1 tipoff to Homeland Security about the poison canister in the State Park, originated right there in the park."

"Really? That's very interesting!"

Chapter Twelve

Like the nucleus of a powerful atom, the center space was hot. Ventilation inside the three story stack of fruit boxes was almost nil. It was the ultimate and extreme hiding place.

These were not the little apple boxes seen in grocery stores, but were the huge field crates used by growers to transport their fruit to the cold-storage warehouses. Each box was four feet square and two and a half feet high. When not in use thousands of crates were stored outside under strict fire prevention regulations. Stacks could not exceed thirty feet in height and sixty feet in breadth and had to be separated by minimum ten foot wide aisles.

For nine or ten months out of every year, crates were occupying many acres of otherwise unusable real estate. Row upon row of them appeared in aerial photographs, looking like mid-sized warehouses.

Sometime well after sundown, one box began to move out from the middle bottom row of a stack. It was on well oiled rollers and slid out from the side of a stack located in the middle of twelve others. The crates above it did not collapse because they were supported by hidden sheets of plywood

Pushing the crate was one Albusi Mahk, crawling on hands and knees. He gulped in great breaths of fresh cool air. Confident he would not be seen, he straightened up to his full six foot height and leaving the crate blocking the aisle, he jogged around and between the other stacks, because he needed exercise.

While he was outside, he also needed to relieve himself. No one ever came into this area except occasional drug dealers, but as Mahk sprinted around the outer perimeter, he suddenly became aware of voices somewhere in the complex.

Backtracking, he returned to his center stack in time to see the backs of four teenage kids disappearing around a corner. He quickly ducked back into his hidey hole, pulling the crate in after him.

He was haunted now by the question whether or not they had seen the wayward crate and he knew that he should have pushed it back into place before beginning his exercise routine. It was a mistake that could be fatal, as he had to remain in hiding for three more days until pre arranged transport would take him out of the country.

His local cell organization had been smashed and he needed to survive in order to renew terrorism somewhere else.

Back in the stack of fruit cases, panic attacks plagued Mahk. *Should I flee now, and take my chances on getting out of the country on my own? Perhaps the kids didn't see the crate in the dark, or if the did, wouldn't they think that it had only just fallen from the top of the stack?*

His thoughts ran rampant. *If I leave this hideout, my contacts would never be able to pick me up for my return home.* He thought further, and bitter rage boiled up against that traitor, Hakim. *I think that little weasel turned me in. Why else was the State Park swarming with cops?*

Mahk had been forced to dump the valuable canister of toxins and barely escaped with his life. *I will kill that snake if I ever see him...* In the airless interior of a stack of fruit boxes, Albusi Mahk drifted off to sleep, alone, scared and steeped in internal hatred.

Chapter Thirteen

Breakfast over, Nick and Marty checked in to work at the park precisely at 9:00 AM just as the office opened. Marty conferred with Nathan who told him to call the police right away.

When he finally got through to Anne Lee, he was abruptly told that police knew all about Hakim's whereabouts in the Park and for Marty to "Keep his nose out of it."

"Well!" he complained to Angie, "They are like a bunch of chameleons, constantly changing colors; happy and thankful for help one day, and all wrapped up in themselves the next."

Before he finished, the phone was ringing.

"It's Sgt. Lee again, for Marty," said Angie, "She must have second thoughts."

Marty took the phone from her hand, listened briefly, said "No," and hung up.

"What was that all about?" asked Nathan.

"Remember when I told them about the money, and they laughed?" said Marty, "Now, all of a sudden, they believe me and asked if I've found it yet?"

"Are you serious?"

"Yeah, and guess what else?... They know it was a drug deal gone sour and that the money was hidden in a tree cavity."

Nathan sat down so heavily at his desk that his chair creaked under the pressure. He propped his elbows on his desk and held his head, all the while groaning loudly.

Marty recognized a theatrical put-on for what it was, but Angie, thinking he might be ill, jumped up and ran to him.

"I'm alright," he said with a huge sigh, "It's just that I'm getting sick hearing about MONEY. Marty found some money and kept quiet, then he found more money and ended up in the hospital with a near skull fracture.

"I'm facing bankruptcy at home because they don't pay me enough money. Marty can't pay his hospital bills because he doesn't have any money. Beth needs money for medicine. I've had to stab all my friends in the back and fire them because the state took away our money.

"Now all the gangs are at war because of money. And the cops think Marty's money was a myth and laughingly tell him to keep it, but now they want the money back. Money is cursed! The Bible says so!"

"Not to interrupt," said Nick, 'but do you think the police really know where Hakim is hiding, or are they bluffing?"

"Unless they've got a satellite positioning device stashed in his back pocket," said Marty, "there's no way they can pin-point his location, other than the fact that he's somewhere in the twelve square miles of this park."

Nick leaned over and whispered in Marty's ear, "What do you say we go looking for him where we lost him yesterday? There's a couple of places I'd like to check-out."

"And what do we do if we find him?" asked Marty.

"Aw, I know there's a risk, but wouldn't it be neat to show up that smarty Sgt. Lee? Can't we phone in his location without him seeing us?"

It was all the challenge Marty needed. But, there was a problem. Ranger Nathan had an urgent assignment, so their detective work would have to wait.

"Rod and Steve are down at the south landing," Nathan started. "Take a gator and pick them up. I want the four of you to launch both rowboats and move the oil booms down to the lower end of the fishing pond. They should be full of that oily stuff the terrorists dumped and they need to be replaced."

Rod and Steve were the other two all season volunteers. Working together, the four finished the job in less than two hours and Marty invited them to go along on their planned snipe hunt.

Opportunities like this were few and far between; smelling the excitement of the chase, they readily agreed.

On the island, Marty and Nick in the lead, Steve and Rod hanging back about two hundred feet, they started scanning for tracks. The other two volunteers agreed that their woodsman skills were far inferior to Marty and Nick's and that they were only along for muscle in case they were needed.

Their direction of travel was generally northwest, straight to what had been Nick's first hide-out. As they approached closer,

Marty signaled for Rod and Steve to spread out, but keep back and hidden. Marty and Nick snuck up on the vine hut from opposite sides, and sure enough, there was Hakim al Awi sound asleep. It would be like stealing candy from a baby.

"Shall we take him, or call for back-up?" whispered Nick.

"Let's both sit on him while he's sleeping," suggested Marty, "I'll use my Pulaski as a weapon, if needed. You sit on his feet."

As he crawled through the narrow opening, Marty could smell alcohol. Hakim was dead drunk! An empty Vodka bottle lay nearby. They moved swiftly as soon as Nick joined Marty, and at their call, Rod and Steve arrived with rope to tie their hostage.

"Shall I call Ann Lee now, or wait until we get back to the office?" asked Marty.

Rod, in a flash of wisdom said, "If I was you, I'd call the media first, take him back and then call the cops."

"Great idea," said Nick, as they led a very calm and helpless Hakim back toward the main part of the park and the office. Nick couldn't help but notice the change in odor. No longer was the after-shave and fish the predominant smells. Alcohol and unwashed body sweat had taken their place.

Marty called his favorite TV anchor person to report the capture. Then he radioed Nathan they were bringing the fugitive in.

"Do you think there might be a reward?" he asked, half joking.

"I thought I ordered no more talk of money, for at least 24 hours," kidded Nathan. "How far out are you?"

"About ten minutes away from the gators, then another five to the office."

"The police and the press should be here when you arrive, ten-four?"

"See you then! Marty out."

#

Peen and Leo had been warned by their Dusty Panthers underground connections to keep out of the local state park. It was rumbled that Rangers and State Police had issued an all points for Peen's old flower Volkswagen van.

Their deep rooted obsession against "people of color" was so strong that they ignored the warning. Logic, however, did dictate use of a different vehicle, which they obtained in a convenience store parking lot where some careless shopper left an engine running while buying beer.

There had been mention of a possible political rally for an NAACP candidate to be held outdoors in the state park, and Peen Hatchet and Leo Leonart had been waiting months for just such an opportunity. This could be their crowning achievement. Their ingrained hatred was further fueled by their conceived dream of the notoriety and fame if they could successfully murder dozens of 'inferior' people.

Thus it was that they were parked near a cluster of outdoor shelters, two well-oiled AKA's at the ready and blood-lust on their minds. An escape plan was in place and included a car switch.

Everything was at the ready. They waited three hours while the western sun drifted towards afternoon.

Nearby ball courts and playground began filling with people and still no sign of any political gathering. Peen moved the vehicle deeper into the park three times when kids began to gather too close for his comfort. The last move took them to the dead-end of the road where a couple of park gators were the only vehicles in the small parking lot.

"Let's just sit here outa sight for awhile," suggested Leo,

"Turn on the noon news while I relieve myself in yonder bushes."

Before he could finish zipping up his fly, Peen was pounding on the car horn, summoning Leo to hurry back.

"Sonofabitch," he growled, "The rally was at Ox-Bow State Park, twenty miles the other side of town!"

Two very angry and disappointed racists sat in the car a while longer considering their next move, when Peen's scowl turned into a wicked smile.

Marty, Nick, Steve and Rod just broke out of the brush, leading one very placid Hakim

"Looky there!," he pointed up the trail. "It's three old men and a little kid, and it looks like they've caught themselves a Muslim."

"Let's take him away from them," said Leo. "Shall we kill him here or take him hostage?" He reached for his automatic rifle.

Chapter Fourteen

The month of March turned into a whirlwind of events that Marty regretted ever having been responsible for starting. For days on end, the park swarmed with satellite trucks from every major network. Every facet of operations of the park was examined, discussed and reenacted in interviews.

Nathan felt like he and his under-funded staff had been put under a high powered microscope.

Reporters were poking into everything, including the budgetary layoffs. Questions surfaced that State Senators could not answer, and some news media began putting pressure on the State Legislature demanding a full disclosure about the reasons for so many layoffs and service cutbacks.

Marty and his volunteer crew were interviewed by every conceivable media;

including the big ones like CNN, Fox and MSNBC. Every day phone calls or mail delivery contained offers for free transportation to New York City or Hollywood to appear on talk shows like Oprah or Hiraldo. If they would write it up, there were even offers of book deals.

Marty wondered why publishers always offered book contracts only to celebrities, especially when they had no writing skills at all. Daily, Marty prayed that the question of the money he had lost from the tree cavity would not come up, and so far, he was spared that embarrassment.

Of course, the amazing tackle of Jason "Peen" Hatchet by two feeble old men in park volunteer uniforms was picked up by National networks and aired across the country on the six o-clock news. Another old man and his 8-year old sidekick were hailed as heroes for going ahead on their own against police advice and tracking down the terrorist Hakim al-Awi and effectively capturing him.

The press had even interviewed Bess at home, inquiring into dumb things like, "What did you feed these heroes that morning for breakfast" and all kinds of other ridiculous questions.

There was little chance that truth would ever be allowed to burst the media bubble. Reporters were told that Hakim was drunk and wanted to be captured, but where's the romance, human interest or bravado in that? Consequently, it was no surprise that the actual truth was never reported.

The International spotlight on the park and its internal financial problems was making certain State Representatives and Senators very nervous. More and more reporters were taking pot shots and a second look behind the narrow passage of the Senate Bill which had cut funding only in "certain" specified parks.

Questions were surfacing to locate why the park budget was suddenly overturned in favor of some County special interests. New Hearings were scheduled. Politicians were squirming.

Hakim was grateful to have escaped the neck-tie party planned for him by Peen and Leo. He told police reporters that he really wanted to be captured, but nobody listened. But when he suggested that he knew where Mahk might be hiding, they sat up and took notice.

Police Sgt. Anne Lee wasn't talking much to anybody, and had turned the whole affair over to Homeland Security chief, Admiral James Lincoln. It became more and more apparent that Hakim was not the bad guy, and the police were having a hard time finding legitimate reasons to hold him

Originally, he had been wanted as a witness to the Homeland Security agent murder in the campground shower building, but the best case they could make against him was possible auto theft.

Hakim was fully cooperative and agreed to testify against Albusi Mahk. He told agents all he knew about terrorist cell exit and entry routes into and out of the country.

There was an ingenious "underground railway" by which they moved. He felt no remorse about exposing his ex-comrades-in-arms. He had never really been a terrorist in the fatal sense if the word. If anybody ever earned leniency for cooperating with authorities, it was Hakim al-Awi. He applied for asylum and was allowed to remain in the United States.

Peen and Leo were charged with the murder of the John Doe who stashed the drug money and were hauled away to some

Federal interment facility and simply disappeared off the face of the earth.

Lawyers for the Dusty Panthers joined forces with lawyers from the A.C.L.U. and tried to find them to post bail, but were stonewalled.

The State's Environmental Toxicology Laboratory took weekly samples of the sludge picked up by the daily movement of the spill booms on the fishing pond and the latest test results were encouraging.

"Maybe we can get a trout implant in time for the opening of fishing season?" It was a hopeful question by Ranger Nathan.

The Chief biologist for Fish and Game studied the reports before him and replied, "It's possible, but only if the toxin levels drop by another twelve parts per million."

Animated, Nathan said, "Well, we cleaned it up sufficiently to drop more than ten p.p.m. in one week, surely twelve more can be extracted in three weeks?"

"Good luck, then," the biologist replied, "I'll request a tanker full of eight to nine inch rainbows to be available for you about March 25th."

"You know that pond was once a deep quarry and some of it is still over 200 feet deep," said Nathan. "Is there any chance that some of our deeper wildlife survived the toxins?"

"You mean like old Walter?"

"Yeah!" Old Walter was the legendary 25 pound Cutthroat trout that folks had tried to catch for the past many years.

"That compound the terrorists dumped is new to us, so anything is possible. But, most of the toxins bonded to the oil carrier and floated to the surface," replied the Fish and Game man, "and your daily attention to the booms has certainly helped."

As he turned to leave, he hollered back over his shoulder, "And, by the way, do you want us to bring you any beaver?"

"No, thank you," said Nathan, "Beaver cause enough damage to my trails, besides which they will migrate in from the river and repopulate on their own soon enough."

A little known fact is that beaver often burrow under water then up into the pond embankment, which sometimes caves-in to form a sink-hole right in the middle of a foot trail. Park staff often has to haul wheelbarrows full of crushed rock or gravel up to half a mile to fill holes in hiking trails.

Planners always survey trails back at least twenty feet from beaver water, but shortcut hikers and fishermen soon wear a new trail along the water's edge.

Back in the park office, Nathan was the happiest Angie had seen him in months.

"We're getting our pond back in a couple weeks. Hallelulia!"

# # #

The joy so apparent in the park was sadly missing in the home of Marty and Beth Bart. A month after Hakim's capture, the TV cameras had all gone, and there were only memories of all the excitement and notoriety.

Attorneys, hired by the park, advised Marty that interview moneys offered by the networks, would be counted as salary and could cause a decrease in his fire department pension, administered by the state. It was good advice, but tended to continue Marty in near poverty.

Worst of all, the Judge overseeing the welfare of Nicholas Fix, decided all the publicity was not good for an impressionable youngster, and ordered temporary foster care in another state.

Bess' tendon swelling worsened and she was confined to a wheelchair. To top it all off, the hospital had turned Marty's account over to collection and they were hounding him to make larger payments. Considering bankruptcy merely added to his depression.

Whenever he hurt, Bess was always there to console.

"Listen to today's Bible lesson," she said, "Let me read it to you from Habakkuk 3:17:

'Though the olive crop fails

and the fields produce no food,

though there are no sheep in the pen

and no cattle in the stalls,

yet I will rejoice in the Lord,

I will be joyful in God my Savior.'"

"It doesn't say anything about Family Court Judges making wrong decisions about Nick," he complained.

"Maybe," she reminded him, "But he'll be back home in a week."

"And that will be a real blessing," said Marty. "I've missed the little cherub. He makes me feel like a kid again."

"I know, she said, "it shows."

"Thanks, love." He kissed her and made sure she had everything handy that she would need for the eight hours he would be working in the park. "You call me now, if you need anything, promise?" Satisfied with her nod, he headed off to work.

When Marty entered the park office, the first thing he noticed was Nathan's infectious smile. And the second thing was a goofy bright green hat on Nathan's head.

"Why the long face?" asked Nathan.

"I guess it's the letdown after all the excitement," suggested Marty, "But the old wolf is still growling at the door."

"Bill collectors, huh?"

"Yeah," growled Marty, "But why are you bursting with happiness?" Nathan had a glow and a smile visible from a mile away and Marty could sense his joy the moment he entered the office.

"Faith 'n begora,' mused Nate, "Sit ye down me lad and I'll share me pot 'o gold with ye."

"Whoops! I forgot all about St. Patrick's Day."

"'And also me birthday," reminded Nate, "And I've just received the best present ever."

Before Marty could ask, Nathan continued, obviously bubbling over with enthusiasm. "The Senate Committee had its hearing yesterday, and unanimously recommended the return of all our funding, plus more. The full Senate has yet to approve it, but the Governor tells me that it's a shoe in."

"That's great news," said Marty, smiling for the first time that day.

Chapter Fifteen

Unknown to Park staff, Metro Police had a good grip on this situation long before any visual sighting was reported of the approaching rival gangs. Units were strategically placed to intercept the rumble, no matter which way the participants headed. It was almost certain, however, their destination would be the State Park.

"Told you so," chided Anne Lee to the driver of her command vehicle, as dispatch relayed the frantic call from Angie.

Sergeant Anne Lee had just been promoted to Lieutenant and this was to be her first high command assignment. On the outside, she appeared confident in her new role, but inside she trembled with fear, and that old insecure, inferiority feeling returned.

"Let the Panthers gather," she commanded, "We'll keep back until the

Norteños get inside the park, then bottle them all up together. Don't anybody move until you get my order."

# # #

Dusty Panthers head-honcho Sidney "Snakes" Sneath had plans to meet the local Red Norteños gang in order to form a compact and a truce. True, many of the Reds were Hispanic or of other questionable blood, according to the Panthers Code, but times were changing and new alliances were needed. Snakes and ten of his most loyal storm troopers were on a peaceful mission, intending to parley.

The State Park had been chosen for its open spaces and solitude. They arrived, and parked outside the front gate, leaving all outward sign of weapons in their vehicles.

"We walk," said Snakes, "It's the only sure way to show the Reds that our intentions are peaceful."

"But, aren't they 'men of color' we are pledged to destroy?"

"Yeah, but this truce is only temporary. We build a comfortable trust first, then we can always change the plans." Snakes made sure that everyone caught the evil gleam in his eye.

Meanwhile, two cars arrived from the opposite direction, six men to a car. They parked near a back trail access, planning to hike around the fishing pond, almost a mile to the rendezvous.

Fidel Ricardo Camacho, their leader was shaken and visibly nervous as he assembled his men.

"How can we be sure about trusting these Aryan Nazis?" he asked. The Neustra Familia have been deadly enemies with the Aryan Brotherhood throughout the entire continent and for too many years to remember."

"Si, but these Skinheads are a splinter group and live by their own rules," replied a member, "We meet with them, then decide the trust issue."

"Okay, let's march," said Camacho, "Remember point one of our creed is to 'Let nothing ever surprise you, and to be alert and aware of your immediate surroundings at all times and in all places.'"

Norteños have never established subsets south of a line drawn through middle California. Many Norteños claim that the area is undesirable. Although Southern California statistically has a warmer climate, a larger economy and several renowned cities; it is also crowded and gang infested.

Social services are stretched to the limit. Ironically the latter concerns are often the primary reason for southern Latinos migrating away from the South to other areas, with the creation of Sureño allied youth gangs in these new areas being a side effect.

Another theory is that geographic expansion is not one of the Norteño's primary concerns; yet Norteño sects can be found in Utah, Arizona, Florida and Illinois. It would seem that establishing a presence outside of California may be more important to Norteños than the attainment of any Southern California rival territory.

However it is more likely that Norteños have not yet penetrated Southern California simply due to the immense numbers of Sureños (in L.A. numbering more than the Crips and Bloods combined) who have been embedded in Southern California neighborhoods for many generations).

Lt. Lee's first screw-up was to assume that both groups would enter the park through the front gate. The Norteños had almost completed their mile long walk before she learned of their arrival through the backside of the park.

"All units," she hollered into her radio, "Proceed at once to Volleyball Court No. 6. The Norteños are already there. Move it and standby!" Police units, mostly teams of two on foot were well hidden in brush at strategic locations throughout the park.

Officers were in full combat gear and as they ran toward the playground area, presented a terrifying spectacle to anyone who saw them.

Mothers scooped up their children in frightened shock and dashed screaming to their cars. To add to the din, three police cruisers and a SWAT van screamed in through the front gate.

Anne Lee had already been hidden behind a hedge a few feet from Volleyball Court #6. Three other officers were with her, all decked out with flak vests and helmets. Each of them carried an M4 rifle and a holstered Glock 40.

What happened next could be encapsulated into a 5-second time frame. Norteños arrived on the scene, heard the sirens, saw armed police running, thought the Panthers had tricked them and pulled hidden weapons to defend themselves.

The Panthers also produced hidden machine pistols, thinking the Norteños had betrayed them, they spread out and ducked for cover behind trees and rocks.

Lieutenant Lee's second screw-up was to draw her sidearm and kick off the safety as she and her contingent jumped out from the bushes. At that same moment the hair trigger felt a slight nervous twitch from her trigger finger and fired.

The opening shot, quite by accident, was sufficient, without any verbal orders, for all three groups to start firing on each other. Fueled by suspicion, a battle royale ensued.

Lee's small group was caught in the crossfire between the two gangs and had to dive for cover. As more cops arrived, they were able to put up a perimeter to protect their commander.

Meanwhile the SWAT light armored vehicle drove a wedge between the two opposing groups, and the battle ended almost as quickly as it started.

Fire paramedics and ambulances were dispatched and set up their triage in the middle of the blood soaked sand volleyball court.

Five Norteños were dead including Camacho, three others injured, one seriously, and three in handcuffs.

Panthers fared a little better, primarily because the Norteños carried only small caliber pistols. They had one dead,

two injured, three missing and the balance under arrest.

Lt. Lee called for K-9 units to assist in trailing the ones who got away, including their leader, "Snakes" Sneath.

Police suffered only two minor injuries, escaping more serious harm because they were protected by flak vests and other body armor. Lt. Lee was a mess with blood streaming from above her left eye, caused by a wayward chip of concrete. The wound was only superficial and would cause no permanent damage.

Nathan, Dave & Marty, wisely chose to leave the battle strategy to the police, Monday-morning quarterbacking the fray from inside the safety of a cement block restroom building. They arrived now to survey the carnage and to assist in the final cleanup of the area.

When it all settled down, Marty's curiosity was now piqued, and he asked Nathan point blank, "What was it that you were going to tell me that 'would make my day?"

# # #

Nicolas Fix put the phone back onto its cradle, and turned to Mrs. Smith with a grin that spread from ear to ear. Evelina Smith had been his temporary court-appointed foster mom for the past month and she said, "What is it, dear?"

"That was the Judge," replied Nick, "and he has released me to go back to Marty and Beth, whenever it is convenient. He's writing up orders that they will be my permanent foster parents until I'm eighteen."

"I assume you want to go?" she asked. "You are a sweet lad, and I've so enjoyed having you here. Do you want to call Martin Bart for transportation, or would you like me to take you and surprise them all?"

"Oh, would you?" pleaded Nick.

"Of course! It's only a three hour drive and we'll leave first thing in the morning."

# # #

Albusi Mahk was mad, so mad that he couldn't think straight. Maybe it was also the heat, limited water intake and hardly any food that contributed to his inability to properly appraise his situation. He had been cooped up in the pile of empty fruit boxes for over a week, five days longer than the escape plan called for.

It was becoming more and more obvious to him that the 'underground railway' of his terrorist organization must have fallen apart. They should have rescued him days ago and he should have been back in his homeland by now. If he was to survive, he knew now that he would have to leave this hideout and strike out on his own.

He knew he was pictured on the most wanted lists and that his chances of escape were next to none. He might be able to make it to the coast, but getting through Customs and Immigration would be another matter.

After dark, the wheeled box was pushed out of the pile for the last time, and a beardless and skinnier man disappeared into the night.

# # #

"This is one birthday I'll never forget," observed Nathan, as the last ambulance and police car left the park.

"C'mon, mean old boss," said Marty, "You can do better than that."

"Okay, lad," started Nathan, "Let's go back to the office, and I'll give you the straight of it. I think you will like what I have to say."

Marty replied with a grin, "Okay, just don't call me lad. I'm old enough to be your grand-father."

They settled down in the office, served a cup of steaming hot coffee by Angie. Marty was beginning to be annoyed by Nathan's 'Cheshire Cat' smile. "Okay, I'm ready... Spill it."

Nathan began, "Straight to the point, your share of the reward money plus Network interview payments has been pooled into a special account to be used for your first hospital expenses, relating to the tree fall."

Marty remembered that State Industrial failed to honor that claim, because it didn't relate to assigned duties in the park. "How much money is there?" asked Marty.

"Enough! And with some left over. But, there's more," continued Nathan, "State Industrial insurance is picking up all expenses of your second hospital visit because your bout with *hunta virus* was contracted while you worked for the park."

Marty sighed, "Then, that means..."

Nathan interrupted, "Yep, ALL your hospital bills are paid in full! And you can have the pleasure of telling those collection agency people to get lost."

"Well now," laughed Marty, "Are you going to lift your restriction yet to talk about money?" Both men laughed.

"See," said Beth, when Marty arrived home and explained their good fortune, "I told you so. God always comes through for those who have faith and love Him. We just can't understand His time-table. Once you told the truth about the money, good things started to happen."

"You are so right, as usual," confessed Marty, "My faith is always made stronger. I just can't wait to see what He plans to do about the lost tree money."

"Remember, Nick comes home next week. Maybe he can help you find a clue."

Marty stretched out in his favorite recliner intending to read the evening paper. Beth was putting away the dinner dishes. The events and the news of the day had left Marty exhausted, and he closed his eyes for a brief nap. Before he could doze, however, that nagging feeling returned. It was his recurring feeling that something very obvious was being overlooked. What could it be? Was he running away from something, or was something, or somebody, running away from him?

Chapter Sixteen

It was Saturday, a day Marty always enjoyed using to catch up on sleep. He was looking forward to a couple of extra hours. The previous day's rumble in the park had been exhausting and Marty was still asleep at ten o'clock. Then, through the pale yellow vapors of the half-sunlight dream, Marty heard a familiar voice.

"Hey, old man, wake up!" It was Nick, "They let me come home five days early. "

It was a stimulant better than hot coffee. Marty was instantly awake. His surprised demeanor of instant shock resembled a sleeper cruelly aroused by being doused with a bucket of ice water. But, it brought the response of instant laughter.

"Nick, little buddy," Marty was out of bed in a flash, "Give me a hug! How'd you get here? Did they treat you well? Are you feeling okay?"

"One question at a time, old man," Nick teased. "Mrs. Smith brought me up and yes and yes. She's out in the kitchen and Beth is feeding her breakfast. Get yourself dressed and join us."

That afternoon, after Evelina Smith returned home, Marty brought Nick up to speed on all that had happened the previous week. They both had excellent news to share; Marty that the hospital bills were covered, and Nick that legal papers were being drawn up awarding foster care to Marty and Beth until Nick's emancipation.

"God is good," remarked Marty, knowing that he now had the responsibility to mentor Nick, both in morals and in faith. It was a happy time for all; Marty had a new challenge and Nick a new future to look forward to.

The next day, after church, Nick took Marty by surprise; he was sitting very still with eyes closed, looking like he was in a trance. When he furrowed his brow, Marty could stand it no longer.

"Are you praying?" he asked

Nick opened his eyes and smiled, "Nope, just thinking."

"What about?"

"If we concentrate and get a little help," replied Nick, "I think we can find your missing money. Then Beth can try out that new tendon treatment we've been hearing about."

"Well, that's a pure motive if I ever heard one." Said Marty, "So, what have you got in mind?

Nick's eyes lit up with the challenge and he said, "Come on, I'll show you." Nick led the way over to the park, a couple of blocks away.

Marty had to use his key to get into the office, and quickly disarm the alarm system. The office was normally closed and locked on Sunday, as all on-duty rangers and aides should be patrolling campgrounds and day-use playgrounds.

Nick led the way into the map-room where there was a large portable blackboard. Chalk in hand, he told Marty to sit facing the chalk-board.

"Now I want you to tell me everything about the night you found the money. Don't leave out anything. Even the smallest detail can be important."

Marty, age 75, couldn't help wise-cracking, "And who taught this smarty pants 8-year old how to do this?"

"I'll be nine in three weeks," answered Nick. "Now concentrate!"

Quite systematically, as Marty recalled, Nick wrote a long list, using the penmanship of a much older boy, occasionally asking questions like, "Did the sun's warmth wake you up under the tree?" Or, "How did you call for help?" Each question generated more thought, reminding Marty of details forgotten, and the list in Nick's neat handwriting grew longer.

"Now let's talk about the money itself," prompted Nick. "Were the bundles tied with string or rubber bands?"

"Bands of paper like the banks use."

"All three?"

"No, one was torn away, but the bills were stuck together anyway."

"Did you pick up all three at once or one at a time?"

"One at a time because my other hand was holding a flashlight."

Nick continued his interrogation, "Where did you put the first packet?

"In my left vest pocket."

"Vest? What vest?"

"You know, my uniform volunteer vest."

Nick showed surprise, "No, I didn't know. You never told me that you had a vest. What color was it?"

"Bright green," answered Marty, perplexed.

"Aha!" exclaimed Nick, a twinkle in his eye, "Tell me again what you felt when you first woke up under the tree." Nick had been grilling Marty on this same thing, by returning to it time and again.

And Marty was beginning to recall things forgotten. "I felt moisture and warmth on my face," his memory suddenly refreshed.

Nick's next question seemed totally out of place. He said, "When was the last time you visited the fox den?"

"Wha-a-at?"

"That's it!" exclaimed Nick, "I remember seeing a green cloth inside the mouth of the fox den. She's got your vest! Why didn't you tell me sooner that you were missing a green vest? If what you told me about feeding her kits is true, that vixen is your friend. She would lick your face while you were unconscious on the dike, and probably took the vest because it had your scent on it.

"I remember now," said Marty. "I was delirious that morning, but now I remember seeing the fox and her two kits walking away from me before I felt around for my cell phone to call for help. It's the vision I've been trying to recall. I even remember now that from the backside I could see the sex of the two kits. They were both males. It's all so clear now."

"Well, what are we waiting for?" Nick was first out the door.

In spite of his excitement, Marty was still the conscientious volunteer. "Wait up!" he hollered, "I've got to set the alarm and lock the place up."

# # #

Alone, hungry and a fugitive, Albusi Mahk could not understand why Allah had abandoned him. After all, his cause was just, or was it? It had not yet occurred to him that perhaps he had misinterpreted the passages in the Quran about jihad.

He was reminded about Ishmael, the son of Abraham and Hagar who was made an outcast along with his mother. This glorious ancestor would be the father of what would later become the Muslim nations. *So, I am an outcast!* His thoughts of comparison with Ishmael were all the motivation he needed to keep him going. Ishmael in Arabic translates to "God hears."

###

Mahk, in his effort to slip undetected out of the state, hot wired a parked car. Without money, he soon had to abandon it when the gas tank ran dry. Rolling a drunk or two corrected that problem.

Stealing clothes off a clothesline had been the easy part of his plan to hide his identity.

Shaving his black beard had already been accomplished while he was living in the pile of apple boxes, so all Mideast demeanor had been deleted. That sweatbox environment had removed almost 40 pounds from his frame. That alone was his best disguise. He felt sure that nobody would recognize him.

Two state-lines later, his confidence increased and he began to relax a little. But relaxation breeds carelessness and he took a chance using a credit card.

His destination was a remote lumber camp in Northern Minnesota a short distance from the Canadian border. It was the last leg of the pre-planned escape route established by the terrorist network for fugitives such as him. The only access was by a narrow gauge railway that hauled the logs out three times a week.

From the camp, he could walk into Ontario and there find a safe house and help to get him through Canadian customs.

Albusi Mahk's trail was followed easily by Homeland Security agents, who knew where he was headed and how he would get there, thanks to Hakim al Awi's courage and cooperation.

So, when he arrived at the Minnesota Lumber mill to locate the train to the lumber camp, agents watched him climb on the rods under an empty flat-car. Their plan was to stop the train and capture him at a remote crossing where no bystander would be hurt if there was any gun play. But, true to his beliefs, Mahk resisted capture and died in a violent gun battle with American agents.

Only in death would Albusi Mahk learn the truth about the insurgency and Jihad martyrdom and if he would or would not be rewarded with the fabled 72 virgins.

Meanwhile, Hakim was now working for the Lebanese Mosque school and continued to pinpoint active terrorist connections, earning much gratitude from law enforcement. His valuable information resulted in many arrests and virtually wiped out all cells in the area. As long as he didn't have to publicly testify at trials against any of his former peers, the source of information would remain hidden

Chapter Seventeen

It was a beautiful spring day when Marty and Nick approached the dike in order to cross over it to the vicinity of the fox den. Anticipation was running high, and Nick was far out ahead when Marty called out, "Slow down, little buddy, this old body can't keep up with you."

Nick climbed up onto the dike and stopped to wait, while Marty caught up, panting heavily. "Let me catch my breath," he pleaded, "Give me a minute or two."

Marty was slightly dizzy and experiencing a pain in his chest. He was sure it was simply a combination of over exertion coupled with higher anticipation. Taking deep breaths, he continued, "What's the rush? The money has been lost and we hope, safely hidden for well over four months, so what difference can a few more minutes make?"

Looking around, Marty made another observation, "We are standing on the exact same spot where the tree fell on me. And over there's the stump of the tree." He pointed back the way they had just come, about twenty feet from the dike.

The stump had been chain-saw cut only two feet above the ground and had a hollow rotted out center almost as big as the diameter of the tree itself.

Another forgotten memory jumped into Marty's brain, something he had never mentioned to anyone because he thought it totally irrelevant. In the cavity before the tree was cut up and hauled off, he remembered finding a tarot card in a zip-lock bag. Somewhere, he had totally lost the card, but remembered now that it was "the hanging man".

It had been many weeks since Marty had visited this spot, and situational *deja vu* generated a new burst of memory. He thought he could feel the foxes wet warm tongue licking his face, and then recalled the admiration he felt watching the fox and her two kits walking away from him that fateful morning. His mind's eye vision was from ground level and the green of his missing vest was now quite visible, held in the teeth of the mother fox. He shook his head and returned to the present.

"Yes, I remember clearly now," he said, pointing, "and that's the direction they went, right toward their den." Marty heaved a huge sigh of relief; his haunting lapse of memory was over, at last.

"Told you so," replied Nick. "Let's go see."

Thunder rumbled ominously on the horizon, signaling the approach of a severe spring storm. It was another flash of *déjà vu*.

Slower this time, they preceded another couple hundred yards to a faint trail that went down the opposite side of the dike toward the river and the island. In a dense grove of teasels, they stood briefly, listening for any sign of life. The foxes den was a network of five or six tunnels in a dirt mound about fifteen feet in diameter.

Neither Nick nor Marty had visited here for several months and they were horrified to see the closest tunnel entrance caved in. Fresh boot tracks showed in the soft earth. Circling the mound, the next tunnel also appeared to be unused as the entrance was full of wind-blown trash and cobwebs.

"Here's where I saw the green cloth," said Nick, as they walked around to the next opening. There they caught an unmistakable pungent smell, a positive indicator the den was still occupied. The odor is common among many small mammals, especially foxes, badgers and skunks, usually derived from a scent gland located near the base of the tail, primarily used for marking territory.

"She's still in residence," declared Marty, "the young kits should have moved out to establish their own territory, by now." "But, where's the vest, and is the money still in it?"

Under an umbrella of beginning panic, Marty and Nick carefully searched all entry to the fox den. Looking into a dark hole in the bright light of day is difficult enough without a flashlight, but Marty showed Nick a special trick he had learned using the crystal face of his wristwatch lined up with the sun, a bright reflection could be aimed into the dark area, just as effective as any flashlight.

But, there was no sign of any green cloth material visible in any of the remaining open tunnels. Nick and Marty's appreciation and love of the environment certainly would not allow them to attempt digging out anything that might be buried thus destroying the habitat.

"What do we do now, boss?" chided Nick.

The answer came from the sky, as fast as if I light switch was turned off. Darkening clouds moving swiftly from the south, blotted out the sun, and seemed to reply to the question with a sudden brilliant flash and a crash of ominous thunder.

Sudden showers by this type common in the Midwest will produce a real deluge; some call them by the name cloudburst. This one was generously mixed with nickel sized hailstones and they were instantly wet. Marty and Nick were hard pressed to find shelter and by the time they reached one of the picnic enclosures in the park, they were drenched and a little bruised.

Then in the distance, they could hear tornado warning sirens signaling the approach of more problems.

The thought occurred to Marty that maybe God was scolding him for every time he got anywhere near this money. Maybe the blood money belonged to Satan?

A fast moving funnel cloud was visible and it was bearing straight down on them. Marty said, "The nearest restroom is concrete block construction, and we'd better make a dash for it."

As they ran again into the deluge, wind whipped the overhead trees causing the release of many branches, some large enough to cause severe damage to a man. It was a frightening time, and became more-so when the roar of an approaching freight train added to the cacophony.

The tornado struck with full fury mere seconds after they reached the restroom building.

"Duck down inside one of the stalls," commanded Marty.

"Someone's already in this one," shouted Nick above the roar. Just then the lights went out and they were plunged into total darkness.

# # #

Hakim al Awi was a highly educated man; one could almost put him into the 'genius' category. It took a high degree of intelligence to engineer the chemical components necessary to manufacture the weapons of mass destruction required of him in his previous role. Now, he was exposed only to the good side of humanity; his soul was at peace; immersed in a life of virtue and kindness.

The Lebanese Mosque School was quick to discover his potential and soon he was teaching college level philosophy along

with a type of apologetics, attempting to prove the validity of the Quran. They paid him a fabulous salary, one that he had no need for.

Research also included real apologetics, having to do with the defense and proofs of Christianity. There, he found unresolved conflicts that he could not explain. A new hunger for answers was born.

Hakim had yet another yearning. His underused intelligence demanded challenge and he felt that he should want to be able to solve the deepest mystery, if furnished with only meager clues. He was always looking for an opportunity to test his mettle.

The meager clues had been shared when he first overheard the skeptic police talking and laughing about Marty's vanished treasure. But there was something in the telling that rang truthful bells in Hakim's makeup. He had been thinking about the mystery for weeks.

Following inadequate clues around the area of the dike, he discovered the foxes den quite by chance. Not realizing the instability of the soft earth, he walked across the mound instead of around it, accidentally caving in one of the tunnels. A green vest bearing the label, 'volunteer' was not on his list of clues, but the content of two bulging pockets was.

Elated at his phenomenal luck, he headed back toward the center of the park to share his good news. He stopped at one of the kitchen shelters to explore the pockets and to count the treasure.

There were three bundles, two banded with bank wrappers, each holding $20,000, and a third bundle that had obviously been very wet and the bills were stuck together like glue. It was smaller and could contain up to an additional $10,000. He didn't want to pull the bills apart for fear of tearing them.

He sat in the vacant shelter for awhile, gloating, but also a little disappointed at how easy it had been; so easy that it destroyed his real challenge. Pure luck had interceded.

At the approach of a fast-moving nasty thunderstorm, he headed in the direction of his parked car. He thought he could outdistance the storm and reach more adequate shelter without getting wet. But the storm was moving too fast. Instead, he ducked into a shower building when he heard the tornado warning sirens.

The concrete walls muffled some of the shriek of the outside storm. It was warm and bright inside and Hakim felt safe, until he felt a sudden change in pressure caused by someone opening the door. He heard a voice say, "Duck down into one of the stalls!" and then the lights went out just before a body fell on him. The sensation of a sardine lasted for only a second until the roar of the storm obliterated all awareness.

A pale daylight returned as the roof peeled away from the building. Cinder block was falling all around as the last of the roof sailed off into oblivion.

The roar abated almost as fast as it began. There was dust everywhere. The storm was over.

Marty was the first to speak, "Nick, are you alright?"

From the adjoining booth, "Yeah, I think so."

"Did you say someone else is there?"

"Yeah, it's Hakim al Awi, and I think he's unconscious."

Marty carefully crawled out from under some twisted metal sheathing and splintered moldings. At the adjoining booth he noticed the metal door completely missing, hinges sheared off. He removed additional debris from Nick who was sprawled on top of Hakim. Hakim was jammed partly behind the stool. He had a bloody gash on his head, apparently caused by one of the falling concrete blocks.

Except for a couple scratches and an ugly bruise on his elbow, Nick was okay, and was removing some of the smaller debris from Hakim. Meanwhile, Marty was on his cell phone, requesting medical assistance.

Apparently the tornado touched down on the floodplain island and tore a very narrow path, uprooting trees, but doing little damage beside the demolished shower room

Medical response was quick in arriving, along with Nathan and Dave. Fire paramedics carefully extracted Hakim who was beginning to stir and show signs of consciousness.

As they loaded him onto the gurney, he called out to Marty, "Did you find your vest?"

The question made no sense to Marty or Nick, who in the excitement, had failed to notice the green volunteer's vest mixed in with the debris of the building.

"Yeah," continued Hakim, "I found the vest and the money in the fox den, and was on my way to tell you." His words faded as they loaded him into the ambulance.

"Well, what d'ya know?" said Nick, "We were right all along."

Back inside the shell of the building, under the block that had fallen on Hakim, they found the vest, pockets bulging, just as he said.

Nathan interrupted, "Outa here, you guys, this building isn't safe."

Safely outside, Marty showed him the vest with part of a stack of $100 bills sticking out of a pocket, "Look what Hakim found."

Nathan whistled and said, "I always thought it really existed.

"But whose is it now? Hakim located it and by salvage law, it belongs to him. Then there's the question of whether or not the police will release it, or hold it for evidence."

Nick's face fell and he said, "So in spite of all our sleuthing, we still have to turn it over to the cops?"

"It would appear that he's right, little buddy," said Marty, "And now the pie threatens to be cut into even smaller pieces by Hakim. I'll bet the police won't even allow us to count it all."

# # #

Three weeks passed without any definitive word regarding ownership of the money. Police did announce the exact amount to

be $48,600. Officials had a good laugh, every time some wannabe-wealthy person concocted some weird story about why they had placed the money in the park and, of course, wanted it back.

The exact amount of money the police released to the media did cause some considerable discussion around Marty's breakfast table.

Adding in the original three-hundred dollars that had starting this adventure, they calculated there must still be more than a thousand dollars missing.

"The squirrel chewed up the first bill," reminded Marty, "and the foxes kits could easily have cut teeth on others."

"Enough of this money talk," scolded Beth, "You can speculate all you want, but when God is ready, you'll have an answer, and not until. Besides all that, today is Nick's birthday."

Nick had been started in the local elementary school, but his intelligence and testing moved him quickly ahead from grade 4 to grade 6. Next year he would advance to Junior High. At the rate he was going, he could be in college by age fourteen.

"No school because of teacher conferences today," announced Marty, "so what would you like to do for your birthday?"

Nick looked a little embarrassed and leaned over to whisper in Marty's ear.

"Really? I think that's a super idea!" I'll let Nathan know that we won't be working today."

Beth felt left out of the conversation and expressed her emotion by clearing her throat and showed a long face.

Marty caught her eye and said, "He wants to go fishing for 'Old Walter'".

Beth smiled, started clearing the breakfast dishes and mumbled, "Just like a man!" She had been getting some cortisone shots and physical therapy and was walking some, grateful to be out of the wheelchair.

"Wanna go with us, hon?" asked Marty, secretly hoping she would say 'yes' but knowing full well that she wouldn't.

It was still early and the sunlight had not yet reached the placid surface of the fishing pond. Shadows of tall trees still covered all but the western end. The water was smooth as glass and a light mist drifted lazily across the surface. Here and there were dimples where newly released trout were feeding on a topside hatch of new wood nymphs. Dragonflies and damselflies were zipping around feasting on a few hapless mosquitoes.

The geese and ducks had returned. When Marty and Nick broke through the trees at the end of the trail, the waterfowl saw them and began moving away, generating ripples that would soon obliterate the polished mirrored surface.

In the distance, they heard the slap of a beaver tail warning others of their intrusion.

"Do you suppose old Walter heard that alarm?" joked Nick.

Song birds were singing to announce the beginning of a beautiful day. The first rays of the rising sun spilled over the tree tops and kissed the surface of the pond's center. The mists quickly evaporated, the day brightened and began to warm.

Nick chose a deep trolling lure from his tackle box, with no advice from Marty. Both knew the pond was open only to juveniles age thirteen and under. Marty agreed that Nick needed no counsel on how to fish.

"Good choice," he commented, "Too big for the smaller trout." It would be a day of physical exertion for the young angler.

Big old fish like Walter were not easily fooled and Nick would have to cast and recast in order to keep his lure moving like a deep diving frog. Such deep trolling had the potential of snagging on bottom debris and loss of many lures.

If the giant trout were to be fooled, it would have to be done very deep, perhaps even near the 200 foot deep bottom.

And, it worked! On the fourth cast, a mighty tug on the line caught Nick off balance and almost pulled him into the water.

It was an exhausting fight but Nick was too proud to ask for help from Marty. Besides which, Marty couldn't legally assist because of his age.

The struggle between two powers on opposite ends of fishing tackle took almost an hour and the boy won, at least so they thought. When the giant fish broke the surface of the now agitated water, Nick and Marty stared at the thing in horror. Marty then broke the rules by plunging out a few feet to assist in landing the object; an object he no longer considered to be in the realm of fish and game laws.

Reaching out for it, Marty had to quell the urge to vomit. What Nick had snagged was a man's arm, with white stringy tendons like material hanging out the end that would have been attached to a torso.

The arm was well preserved because of the depths and the cold of the 200 feet plus pond. Frantically tugging with all his mustered strength, Marty reached ankle deep water, and fell exhausted. He was panting so hard that his wheeze caused Nick concern.

"Are you okay, old man?"

"Wheez... Give me a minute..." Marty was looking at a loop of heavy metal cable that was imbedded in the skin of the elbow joint. After catching his breath, he said to Nick, "That cable is attached to some other heavy object that is still out of sight under the water."

"Shall we pull it out, together?"

"No," replied Marty, "This is now a crime scene and we better leave everything to the police."

Marty made the call on his cell phone, giving dispatch exact instructions to their location. It was still too early for anybody to be in the park office.

Marty tried Nathan's cell phone and home phone, getting no answer at either.

"We wait right here, touching nothing, the detectives told me they are on the way."

Nick frowned at the unexpected interruption of his fishing holiday. "I wonder if old Walter really is still alive?'

It was only coincidental, but Nick today still feels that the fish heard his question. As if on cue, one very large trout broke the surface and rose almost two feet in the air for a large June bug. It fell back with a resounding splat generating huge ripples.

"Did you see that?"

But, Marty was bending down, examining the dead hand. "Looky here," he said, "These gold rings must be worth a fortune." They stared in disbelief at three gold adorned fingers, the largest sporting a huge piece of jewelry that appeared as if it could weigh a half a pound or more. The gold band was almost an inch wide, supporting a spectacular ruby, surrounded by a cluster of twelve diamonds, each one looking to be almost a full carat in size. An Arabic engraving was partially visible.

"But, I just saw Walter!"

"I know. But this looks like something a king or a sheik would wear," commented Marty, "and see the finely woven silk sleeve, definitely of Eastern origin. A simultaneous thought occurred to both, and both mouthed the name at the same time, Mahk...? Or maybe one of his cronies?"

"I wonder what's attached to the other end of that cable." Marty said, "I don't think it will turn out to be Walter."

"Funny," chided Nick.

Sirens were now audible, becoming louder with each passing second.

"They'll be here in a minute or two," said Marty, "then maybe we'll find out."

Uniformed patrolmen were first on the scene, unrolling their limitless rolls of red or yellow "Crime Scene" tape. "You guys sit right where you are," ordered one, "Detectives are right behind us."

Detective Anne Lee and her staff were next to crash through the bushes. Spotting Marty and Nick, she cursed. "Can't you two go build a trail or something and keep out of police business?"

"But, we love you, Anne!" Marty was joking.

An hour later, after dictating several extra reports, Nick and Marty were released. They had watched a portable dredge haul out the other end of the cable. Attached to it was a six and a half foot long cigar shaped cylinder, about two feet in diameter. It had fins resembling a rocket of some sort. It was a hinged pod, but the detectives refused to open it without further lab testing. So Marty and Nick finished the day, sharing more mysteries with Nathan and other park staff.

The questions grew. Where and who was the other part of the body?

What king, prince or other political potentate did the arm belong to? What was in the cylinder? Who went to so much trouble to weigh down a body to stay at such depth and not implode with bodily gas?

Who...?

Later, at the park office, the questions unanswered, all were seeking comfort from each other.

"What a day this has been," said Marty.

Angie called Nathan on the intercom, "Hakim on line two for Nathan."

The name Hakim brought them all back to reality. The fishing trip was over. "I wonder what he wants, besides the money?" said Nick.

Marty clasped Nick on the shoulder and moved him out of the office. "It's Nathan's call, it's none of our business, and I have some good advice for you my boy," he said. "Hakim just got out of the hospital and we can't judge what he may or may not want. The Bible teaches to always think well of everybody; they may surprise you."

Nathan called them back into his office. "Hakim wants to meet with you over lunch," he said, "as soon as possible."

"See," Marty told Nick, "not everyone we think badly of, turns out to be an enemy."

Nick replied, "Yeah, that's a good thought, but many of your friends can turn out to be enemies..."

Chapter Eighteen

The lunch meeting with Hakim was set up for the first day of the following week. Hakim raised suspicions when he requested the meeting with Marty alone. A little worried, Nathan contacted Metro for advice. Detective Anne Lee had been demoted back to sergeant because of her mishandling the gang meeting in the park. She told Nathan, "All charges have been dropped and Hakim al Awi is no longer our concern."

"What about the money?"

"The District Attorney can't find any legal reason to impound it and is going to release it within a couple of days." Anne Lee turned away, indicating the conversation was at an end, then paused and continued, "Ownership will have to be worked out between Hakim and Marty."

"I know," pleaded Nathan, "but isn't there some way you can put Hakim under surveillance, off the record?"

"You and your rangers have all been through the police academy," she countered, "why can't you take care of it?"

"Hakim knows all of my people, and he asked Marty to come alone."

"Any idea what he wants?"

"Obviously something to do with the money," said Nathan,

"Does he know of the DA's decision?"

"No, and you don't either, if you get my meaning," warned the Sergeant, "and personally, I don't trust him, either. I'll see what my Captain says."

# # #

Beth's doctors had been given the go-ahead to begin tendon reconstruction, because Marty now felt it could be done without bankrupting them. The money awarded for TV interviews had been squirreled away into a special trust fund.

Their lawyer had found some obsolete legal loophole to shelter the money from being declared income, but it could only be used for medical services. In that way, Marty's pension would not be affected and the "award" would be exempt from state and federal income taxes.

If he could keep the money from the squirrel's tree, the lawyers hadn't yet figured that out. It would be a windfall no matter how they argued. A local Internal Revenue Service agent already had a watchful eye turned toward Marty Aloyisius Bart.

Beth was feeling on cloud nine. She was given joint injections of some new cortisone based compound by her new physician. They relieved most of her pain and allowed walking with the help of a cane. Her future looked bright because of some new tendon transplant procedures.

The Bart household was also a lot more cheerful. There were many reasons, chief of which was the return to a younger and more active life by Marty and Beth.

The feeling was daily reinforced when they helped Nick with homework, Bible study and school projects. Nick's contributions to this happy family were charismatic. The happy, bubbling boy living in their house brought them out of retirement and made them both feel forty years younger.

Marty and Beth witnessed to the power and love of God each Sunday at their church. People were moved by all the good news they had to share.

When asked how much the State paid them for Nick's foster care, Marty would only smile and say, "I should pay them instead for all the joy caring for Nick brings to us."

# # #

After the big rumble in the park, police K-9 units located two of the three missing Dusty Panthers hiding out in the island area on the other side of the dike. When confronted with the well trained but vicious teeth of the German Shepherds, they surrendered without incident. Days later, there was still no sign of Sidney "Snakes" Sneath, their erstwhile leader. He cleverly eluded police who searched for him in three counties.

Needless to say, there would be frustrated cops if and when it was finally learned he had been hidden right under their noses in the city center, less than three miles from police headquarters.

In all the years Dusty Panthers had occupied the abandoned rail switch tower, it was miraculous that law enforcement never learned of their hideout. On this day, Snakes was the only occupant. All his radical followers were gone; either dead or in jails waiting what would prove to be long sentences. He wondered if they still spewed out their racial hatred slogans.

He could not show his face anywhere without risk of exposure. His money was gone and what little food and booze remained in the hideout would soon run out.

His worst frustrations surfaced when he ran out of cigarettes and could not find a sharp enough razor to shave his head. The more he drank, the more depressed he became, which led to more drinking.

The skinheads' hideout however was not hidden to everyone. Revenge can be a powerful force amongst criminals and so it happened that Snakes was so drunk he did not know a thing when a group of Norteños appeared one night and slipped a blade into his left ventricle. Before leaving, they marked the place on all sides with their sign, XIV using red aerosol paint.

A stench of death would permeate the hideout for months, but there would be no one to smell it, except the birds.

So the police would continue looking for Sidney Sneath alias "Snakes."

Months later, a sharp eyed railroad bull noticed the graffiti on the old switching tower and sent a crew to clean it up.

# # #

Marty was worried. He was on his way to a fancy uptown bar and grille on the top floor of the city's tallest high-rise, 72 floors above the sprawling metropolis. It was the place Hakim, the Muslim had chosen for their luncheon meeting.

Originally, the plan had been to meet in an outdoor garden restaurant in the suburbs called Julianna's. It was well known for its gardens, waterfalls, live cockatoos, colorful parrots and flowering vines and Marty had looked forward to going there. Besides which, observation and surveillance would have been so much easier to hide in the bushes, and to intercept Hakim if he tried anything fishy.

Hakim, however insisted on the last minute change. If one of Metro's detectives was tagging along for protection, Marty had no way of knowing.

As Marty's elevator ascended, an odd thought jumped into his head; *the building had 72 floors... wasn't that the number of virgins jihad martyrs were supposed to be rewarded with?* Hakim had once been willing to die in order to destroy this city. Had he really changed?

Marty's stomach was tied in knots as he exited the elevator and approached the headwaiter. He felt that he would not be able to eat a thing.

Hakim was already there, seated outside on the veranda, with only a five foot glass panel between him and a 720 foot freefall.

Marty gulped. Hakim rose to greet him, sporting a huge smile and extending a frail thin hand. Marty immediately noticed a large and ominous bulge under Hakim's jacket.

"Do you mind sitting somewhere away from the edge," pleaded Marty, "Heights make me dizzy." Then, to soften the moment, he added, "It's my old age, you know."

"No problem," said Hakim, "you are my guest". He moved to a different table. Marty felt a little more at ease. They ordered and ate with very little conversation, other than polite chit chat. Then, Hakim ordered a rich (and very thick) Arabian coffee.

"That is why I chose this place, called Little Egypt. It's the only place in town that knows how to serve real coffee."

Marty tried the bitter thick coffee and again had doubts about his personal safety. He knew Hakim was watching and tried to control his reflexes to keep from gagging. "Very stimulating," he stuttered behind a weak smile.

"About why we are here," Hakim began while stroking the bulge hidden under his vest. Time seemed to stand still for Marty and a cold sweat broke out on this forehead. He thought of excusing himself to the restroom, but not coming back. His fear was most apparent.

Noticing Marty's sudden fright, Hakim laughed, "Relax, I am more of a friend than you know." He proceeded to pull a thick black book out of his vest.

Marty felt extremely foolish when Hakim laid a Bible on the table between them.

Hakim continued, "You are worried about who keeps the money, no?"

"It has crossed my mind."

"It is yours, you keep all." Hakim said, "I want no part of it. I search for you because Hakim needs to be friend."

Marty's mouth fell open.

"One condition," Hakim continued.

"Yes?"

Hakim thumped the Bible. "You teach Hakim all you know about this man, the one named Jesus the Christ."

"Agreed!" replied Marty, with a smile from ear to ear. "Let's have some dessert."

Chapter Nineteen

When the Department of Homeland Security finally released their findings about the grizzly arm piece Nick hooked into, it almost caused an international incident. Newspapers around the world announced:

"Missing Suez Emirate

Ambassador Found Decapitated in USA."

Unreported in the media was the fact the Ambassador was also an undercover agent for the Egyptian Secret Police. Nathan shared this bit of info with his park staff on the condition they tell no one.

What he wanted to share, but couldn't was information about the canister that was tied to the arm. Apparently Nick's mighty tug severed the arm from the torso, because two days later, the rest of the Ambassador's bloated body floated to the surface. The canister was currently under armed guard, quarantined at a Federal laboratory somewhere in Virginia. It was found to contain a brand new toxin contained only by a very unsophisticated release mechanism. A simple tin diaphragm, thin enough to rust away, was all that separated the bio-toxin from contaminating the water and then spreading to the entire state.

According to best estimates, it would have rusted through and released in less than a week.

After Hakim al Awi's unexpected announcement, feelings about him were radically changed. In fact, Marty's ideas about the strong Turkish coffee also changed. He hated the stuff when Hakim first introduced him to it, but now his tastes were changing.

At every opportunity, conversation both in and out of the park, centered on some of the questions that still remained unanswered. At the top of the list was the apparent disappearance of Albusi Mahk.

Everybody felt reasonably certain that Mahk was the perpetrator of the Ambassador's murder and the placement of the second canister. Police gave him credit for providing a surprise backup in case the first one failed, which it did. They estimated the body and the second canister had been in the pond for at least two months.

After Marty explained Christianity to Hakim and provided him with reading material, he seemed to retreat into his teaching at the Muslim School. No one heard anything from him for over a month.

One day, Nathan called Marty into the office. "I just heard they captured Mahk, the terrorist. He was attempting to cross into Quebec, Canada.

"Wow! He made it a long way," said Marty. "Are they bringing him back here for trial?"

"Not likely," said Nathan, "He died in a gun battle with Federal agents."

"Well that leaves three Panthers unaccounted for."

"Oh," continued Nathan, "I forgot to tell you. Somebody wasted Snakes. They found him after the smell of death lead a railroad policeman to the old Panther hideout. It was that unused switch-mans' house in the middle of the rail yard.

"Okay, two down, two to go," said Nick, who had just come into the room on his way home from school.

Nathan looked at him funny like, and said, "Any bright ideas where they might be, Sherlock?"

Everyone laughed, but Nick ignored them. He had ideas of his own.

# # #

Early the next Saturday morning, Marty looked at Nick and said, "Well, are you still interested in fishing?"

"You don't think a dead body scared me off, do you? I'm going to catch that old Walter now, for sure"

"Play it again, Nick!"

But again, it worked! On the fourth cast, a mighty tug on the line caught Nick off balance and almost pulled him into the water. It was an exhausting fight but Nick was too proud to ask for help from Marty. Besides which, Marty couldn't legally assist because of his age.

The struggle between and small boy took almost an hour and the boy won, at least at first. When the fish was landed, Marty took pictures and measured the length at thirty-three and a fraction inches.

No scale was available, but the estimated weight was about twenty-eight pounds.

Panting and hot, Nick carefully removed the lure's hook and the myth was broken when Walter was allowed to return to his deep water home. It was a win-win situation for all concerned.

"I just caught old Walter!" Nick shouted, bursting into Ranger Nathan's office.

"Sure you did! Where's the fish?" Nathan scoffed.

"Really! Marty has pictures."

"Yes I do," said Marty, entering behind Nick, "He's earned his freedom so we released him back into the pond." He handed skeptical Nathan the image on his digital camera.

"What a surprise! Congratulations."

Marty suggested making framed enlargements to hang in the office and

Nathan agreed that would be a splendid idea.

"The myth is finally dispelled and we can prove that he really exists. It's a miracle that he survived all the poison junk the terrorists released there," Nathan added.

"How old do you think he is?" asked Nick.

"Dunno," said Marty, "But he was a legend when I started volunteering, fourteen years ago."

Chapter Twenty

Marty pulled into the church parking lot, noticing many parking spaces were already filled. He slipped his little Toyota in alongside a TV satellite truck and parked.

"Wonder what they are doing here? It's Memorial Day weekend and everybody is usually out of town." he commented to Beth as he opened her door. Out of habit, Marty reached out to assist her in getting out of the low car.

"I can do it myself" she said, "Thank you." Beth had been disabled for so long it was routine habit for Marty to reach out to help her.

"I forgot again," he apologized. "I'm sure grateful to see your strength returning and thank God for a successful surgery."

For a holiday weekend, the Morningstar Pentecostal Church was crowded and Marty wondered why. He was not aware of any special event. After he seated Beth, he reported to the welcome center for his ushering assignment. Signing in, he asked the head usher what was going on.

"We are having water baptism this morning," he replied.

"Yes, I knew that," said Marty, "But why all the extra people and media?"

"My only guess is that somebody important is attending the service," the Head Usher suggested, "but nobody told me who it might be. I haven't seen any Secret Service guards." He winked as he said it.

Marty entered the sanctuary and took up his regular station, greeting and seating people for the soon to begin church service.

To his surprise, Detective Anne Lee and her husband asked to be seated close to the front.

I've never seen her in church before, Marty thought, *Something must be happening.* He also noticed there were a few prominent Jewish and Palestinian community leaders scattered throughout the congregation.

The choir filed out onto the platform to begin the praise service and Marty would soon have an answer. After a couple of rousing, hand-clapping songs, one of the youth pastors called for the water baptisms to begin. There were ten candidates and for each dunking the congregation would cheer. The first six were young converts or members' children who most everybody knew.

When the seventh candidate stepped down into the baptistery pool, Marty gasped in surprise. It was Hakim al Awi! The TV cameramen moved in for close-ups.

"I baptize you, in the name of the Father, the Son and the Holy Spirit," intoned the pastor. When Hakim emerged from the water, the congregation cheered.

Marty felt genuine pride because his protégé was making this commitment. Suddenly, it became crystal clear why all the media was giving the occasion so much attention. Hakim was a convert in more ways than one.

He had been in the national news when labeled a 'terrorist" when Marty and Nick captured him. His brother was one of the perpetrators of the dirty bomb attempt and had died in that attempt. And more than a few knew how his help had wiped out all other area cells. Any time that a hard-core terrorist is truly converted, it makes national news.

Marty really wanted to puff himself up with pride for having discipled Hakim, but resisted the temptation. Another thought bothered Marty. He hoped Hakim would make no mention of his tutoring which would throw the media spotlight back on Marty. He did not want that to happen.

Following Hakim, three other well known Muslims committed to a life with Christ.

# # #

The next day was busy in the state park. Memorial Day was the opening of the summer season and all staff and volunteers were expected to be available for traffic and crowd control.

Nathan expressed pleasure at the news about Hakim and then he set Marty and Nick to staining birdhouses, until they might be needed elsewhere.

Nathan offered birdhouses to friends of the park when they made donations. Park budget had been restored by the Legislature, but any little extras or minor improvements had to be financed by contributions.

It was an easy and pleasant time. Marty enjoyed Nick's company. With Nick in school weekdays, their time together in the park was limited. Nathan provided the boy with a vest and volunteer hat, which he wore with pride.

"It's been a great year for both of us," said Nick, "What are you going to do with the money?"

"After taxes, we only get about $39,000 and I plan to send you to college," answered Marty, "Maybe I should write a book..?"

"If you do, you'll have to explain all the clues, or make something up." Nick laughed at the thought of making things up. Then he continued, "Like that mysterious tarot card that was sealed inside a zip-loc bag. What did you say it was?"

"The hanging man."

"What did it mean?"

"You know," said Marty, "That's the weird thing... It was almost like a prophecy. Tarot is like fortune telling and witchcraft, and Christians aren't supposed have anything to do with it, because it comes from Satan.

Beth was curious and looked it up

on the computer and printed it out for me." He reached into his shirt pocket and unfolded a piece of paper and started reading.

"The Hanged Man is one of the most mysterious cards in the tarot deck. It is simple, but complex. It attracts, but also disturbs. It contradicts itself in countless ways. The Hanged Man is unsettling because it symbolizes the action of paradox in our lives. A paradox is something that appears contradictory, and yet is true. The Hanged Man presents to us certain truths, but they are hidden in their opposites."

"Let me see that for a second," pleaded Nick. He scanned the page, made a tssk sound and then said, "It sounds just like an outline of your whole relationship with the money from the day you first found it."

"Exactly!" exclaimed Marty. "Let me finish reading it. The main lesson of the Hanged Man is that we 'control' by letting go – we 'win' by surrendering. The action of letting go means:

- Having an emotional release
- Accepting what is
- Surrendering to experience
- Ending the struggle

- Being vulnerable and open
- Giving up control
- And ACCEPTING GOD'S WILL

"In readings, the Hanged Man reminds us that the best approach to a problem is not always the most obvious. When we most want to force our will on someone that is when we should release. When we most want to have our own way, that is when we should sacrifice. When we most want to act, that is when we should wait. The irony is that by making these contradictory moves, we find what we are looking for."

"Wow!"

"Wow, indeed," said Nathan, who had walked up unseen and overheard part of the reading. "So this is how you guys lollygag when you're supposed to be working."

"So, dock our pay," laughed Marty.

An hour later, Marty and Nick were going home for lunch, when Nick got serious, "I don't think I have ever known anybody as relaxed as you. Yet, you are always teaching me something valuable and I - I - really love you guys. Thanks for being my family."

Marty blushed, gave Nick a big hug, then changed the subject.

"Beth went to a barbeque with her Bible study group," he said, "so we're on our own for lunch. Do you want an 'over the sink' sandwich, or one you can eat at the table?"

"What d'ya mean?" questioned Nick.

"Pay attention, and learn from the master. I'll create three drippy masterpieces, one for you, one for me and one for Me-Tzu and Precious to share. At the mention of their names, the two dogs bounded into the kitchen, tails wagging.

After a moist drippy lunch shared by all, it was time to go back to the state park.

"Just two questions," said Nick, "If you think the original stash in the squirrel cavity was $50,000 even, what do you think happed to the missing thousand?

"And?"

"Who placed the tarot card in the tree cavity?"

Marty reached out and tousled the boy's hair saying, "Nick, my son, that's a different story that could fill another whole book. Let's get back to work!"

The End